THE LIME TWIG

BY JOHN HAWKES

The Beetle Leg

The Blood Oranges

The Cannibal

Death, Sleep & The Traveler

The Innocent Party (plays)

The Lime Twig

Lunar Landscapes

The Owl

Second Skin

Travesty

Virginie: Her Two Lives

ABOUT JOHN HAWKES:

A John Hawkes Symposium: Design and Debris (Insights-I: Working Papers in Contemporary Criticism)

THE LIME TWIG

BY

JOHN HAWKES

with an introduction by Leslie A. Fiedler

A NEW DIRECTIONS BOOK

Library of Congress Catalog Card No. 60–14719

(ISBN: 0-8112-0065-5)

Portions of this book first appeared in *Accent*, Winter 1960, and *Audience*, Spring 1960.

Manufactured in the United States of America.
Published in Canada by George J. McLeod Ltd., Toronto
New Directions Books are published for James Laughlin by New Directions Publishing Corporation, 80 Eighth Avenue, New York 10011.

FIFTEENTH PRINTING

For Maclin Guerard

The Pleasures of John Hawkes

BY LESLIE A. FIEDLER

Everyone knows that in our literature an age of experimentalism is over and an age of recapitulation has begun; and few of us, I suspect, really regret it. How comfortable it is to be interested in literature in a time of standard acceptance and standard dissent—when the only thing more conventionalized than convention is revolt. How reassuring to pick up the latest book of the latest young novelist and to discover there familiar themes, familiar techniques—accompanied often by the order of skill available to the beginner when he is able (sometimes even with passionate conviction) to embrace received ideas, exploit established forms. Not only is the writing of really new books a perilous pursuit, but even the reading of such books is beset with dangers; and it is for this reason, I suppose, that readers are secretly grateful to authors content to rewrite the dangerous books of the past. A sense of *déjà vu* takes the curse off the whole ticklish enterprise in which the writer engages, mitigates the terror and truth which we seek in his art at the same time we cravenly hope that it is not there.

John Hawkes neither rewrites nor recapitulates, and, therefore, spares us neither terror nor truth. It is, indeed, in the interests of the latter that he endures seeming in 1960 that unfashionable and suspect stereotype, the "experimental writer." Hawkes' "experimentalism" is, however, his own rather than that of yesterday's avant-garde rehashed; he is no more an echoer of other men's revolts than he is a subscriber to the recent drift toward neo-middlebrow sentimentality. He is a lonely eccentric, a genuine unique—a not uncommon American case, or at least one that used to be not uncommon; though now, I fear, loneliness has become as difficult to maintain among us as failure. Yet John Hawkes has managed both, is perhaps (after the publication of three books and on the verge of that of the fourth) the least read novelist of substantial merit in the United States. I recall a year or so ago coming across an ad in the *Partisan Review* in which Mr. Hawkes' publisher was decrying one of those exclusions which have typically plagued him. "Is *Partisan*," that publisher asked, "doing right by its readers when it consistently excludes from its pages the work of such writers as Edward Dahlberg, Kenneth Patchen, Henry Miller, John Hawkes and Kenneth Rexroth?"

But God knows that of all that list only Hawkes really *needs* the help of the *Partisan Review*. Miller has come to seem grandpa to a large part of a generation; while the two Kenneths are surely not without appropriate honors and even Dahlberg has his impassioned exponents. Who, however, reads John Hawkes? Only a few of us, I fear, tempted to pride by our fewness, and ready in that pride to believe that the recalcitrant rest of the world doesn't deserve Hawkes, that we would do well to keep his pleasures our little secret. To tout him too widely would be the equivalent of an article in *Holiday*, a note in the travel section of the *Sunday Times*, might turn a private delight into an attraction for everybody. Hordes of the idly curious might descend on him and us, gaping, pointing—and bringing with them the Coca-Cola sign, the hot-dog stand. They've got Ischia now and Mallorca and Walden Pond. Let them leave us Hawkes! But, of course, the tourists would never really come; and who would be foolish enough in any case to deny to anyone daylight access to those waste places of the mind from which no one can be barred at night, which the least subtle visit in darkness and unknowing. Hawkes may be an unpopular writer, but he is not an esoteric one; for the places he defines are the places in which we all live between sleeping and waking, and the pleasures he affords are the pleasures of returning to those places between waking and sleeping.

He is, in short, a Gothic novelist; but this means one who makes terror rather than love the center of his work, knowing all the while, of course, that there can be no terror without the hope for love and love's defeat. In *The Cannibal, The Beetle Leg*, and *The Goose on the Grave* he has pursued through certain lunar landscapes (called variously Germany or the American West or Italy) his vision of horror and baffled passion; nor has his failure to reach a wide audience shaken his faith in his themes. In *The Lime Twig* he takes up the Gothic pursuit once more, though this time his lunar landscape is called England; and the nightmare through which his terrified protagonists flee reaches its climax at a race meeting, where gangsters and cops and a stolen horse bring to Michael Banks and his wife the spectacular doom which others of us dream and wake from, relieved, but which they, improbably live.

It is all, on one level, a little like a thriller, a story, say, by Graham Greene; and, indeed, there is a tension in *The Lime Twig* absent from Hawkes' earlier work: a pull between the aspiration toward popular narrative (vulgar, humorous, suspenseful) and the dedication to the austerities of highbrow horror. Yet Hawkes' new novel finally avoids the treacherous lucidity of the ordinary shocker, the kind of clarity intended to assure a reader that the violence he relives destroys only certain characters in a book, not the fabric of the world he inhabits. In a culture where even terror has been so vulgarized by mass entertainers that we can scarcely believe in it any longer, we hunger to be persuaded that, after all, it really counts. For unless the horror we live is real, there is no point to our lives; and it is to writers like Hawkes that we turn from the wholesale slaughter on T.V. to be convinced of the reality of what we most fear. If *The Lime Twig* reminds us of *Brighton Rock*, which in turn reminds us of a movie by Hitchcock, it is of *Brighton Rock* recalled in a delirium or by a drowning man—*Brighton Rock* rewritten by Djuna Barnes. Hawkes, however, shares the effeteness of Djuna Barnes's vision of evil no more than he does the piety of Greene's vision of sin. His view avoids the aesthetic and the theological alike, since it deals with the mysteries neither of the world of art nor of the spirit—but only with the immitigable mystery of the world of common experience. It is not so much the fact that love succumbs to terror which obsesses Hawkes as the fact that love breeding terror is itself the final terror. This he neither denies nor conceals, being incapable of the evasions of sentimentality: the writer's capitulation before his audience's desire to be deceived, his own to be approved. Hawkes' novel makes painfully clear how William Hencher's love for his mother, dead in the fire-bombings of London, brings him back years later to the lodgings they once shared—a fat man with elastic sleeves on his thighs, in whom the encysted small boy cannot leave off remembering and suffering. But in those lodgings he discovers Banks and his wife Margaret, yearns toward them with a second love verging on madness, serves them tea in bed and prowls their apartment during their occasional absences, searching for some way to bind them, his memories, and his self together. "I found," he reports of one such occasion, "her small tube of cosmetic for the lips and, in the lavatory, drew a red circle with it round each of my eyes. I had their bed to myself while they were gone." It is, however, Hencher's absurd and fetishistic passion which draws Michael Banks out of the safe routine of his life into crime, helps, that is, to turn a lifetime of erotic daydreaming about horses into the act of stealing a real race horse called Rock Castle.

And the end of it all is sheer terror: Hencher kicked to a pulp in a stable; Margaret Banks naked beneath the shreds of a hospital gown and lovingly beaten to death; Michael, screwed silly by all his nympholeptic dreams become flesh, throwing himself under the hooves of a field of horses bunched for the final turn and the stretch! What each of Hawkes' doomed lovers has proposed to himself in fantasy—atrocious pleasure or half-desired indignity—he endures in fact. But each lover, under cover of whatever images, has ultimately yearned for his own death and consequently dies; while the anti-lovers, the killers, whose fall guys and victims the lovers become, having wished only for the death of others, survive: Syb, the come-on girl, tart and teaser; Little Dora, huge and aseptically cruel behind her aging schoolmarm's face; and Larry, gangster-in-chief and cock-of-the-house, who stands stripped toward the novel's end, indestructible in the midst of the destruction he has willed, a phallic god in brass knuckles and bulletproof vest.

> They cheered, slapping the oxen arms, slapping the flesh, and cheered when the metal vest was returned to him—steel and skin—and the holster was settled again but in an armpit naked now and smelling of scented freshener.
>
> Larry turned slowly round so they could see, and there was the gun's blue butt, the dazzling links of steel, the hairless and swarthy torso. . . .
>
> "For twenty years," shouted Dora again through the smoke opaque as ice, "for twenty years I've admired that! Does anybody blame me." Banks listened and . . . for a moment met the eyes of Sybilline, his Syb, eyes in a lovely face pressed hard against the smoothest portion of Larry's arm, which—her face with auburn hair was just below his shoulder—could take the punches . . .

And even these are bound together in something like love.

Of all the book's protagonists, only Sidney Slyter is without love; half dopester of the races, half amateur detective, Sidney is at once a spokesman for the novelist and a parody of the novelist's role, providing a choral commentary on the action, which his own curiosity spurs toward its end. Each section of the novel opens with a quotation from his newspaper column, *Sidney Slyter says*, in which the jargon of the sports page merges into a kind of surrealistic poetry, the matter of fact threatens continually to become hallucination. But precisely here is the clue to the final achievement of Hawkes' art, his detachment from that long literary tradition which assumes that consciousness is continuous, that experience reaches us in a series of framed and unified scenes, and that—in life as well as books—we are aware simultaneously of details and the context in which we confront them.

Such a set of assumptions seems scarcely tenable in a post-Freudian, post-Einsteinian world; and we cling to it more, perhaps, out of piety toward the literature of the past than out of respect for life in the present. In the world of Hawkes' fiction, however, we are forced to abandon such traditional presumptions and the security we find in hanging on to them. His characters move not from scene to scene but in and out of focus; for they float in a space whose essence is indistinctness, endure in a time which refuses either to begin or end. To be sure, certain details are rendered with a more than normal, an almost painful clarity (quite suddenly a white horse dangles in mid-air before us, vividly defined, or we are gazing close up, at a pair of speckled buttocks), but the contexts which give them meaning and location are blurred by fog or alcohol, by darkness or weariness or the failure of attention. It is all, in short, quite like the consciousness we live by but do not record in books—untidy, half-focused, disarrayed.

The order which retrospectively we *impose* on our awareness of events (by an effort of the will and imagination so unflagging that we are no more conscious of it than of our breathing) Hawkes decomposes. For the sake of art and the truth, he dissolves the rational universe which we are driven, for the sake of sanity and peace, to manufacture out of the chaos of memory, impression, reflex and fantasy that threatens eternally to engulf us. Yet he does not abandon all form in his quest for the illusion of formlessness; in the random conjunction of reason and madness, blur and focus, he finds occasions for wit and grace. Counterfeits of insanity (automatic writing, the scrawls of the drunk and doped) are finally boring; while the compositions of the actually insane are in the end merely documents, terrible and depressing. Hawkes gives us neither of these surrenders to unreason but rather reason's last desperate attempt to know what unreason is; and in such knowledge there are possibilities not only for poetry and power but for pleasure as well.

Goshen, Vermont
June, 1960

THE LIME TWIG

SIDNEY SLYTER SAYS

Dreary Station Severely Damaged During Night . . .

Bomber Crashes in Laundry Court . . .

Fires Burning Still in Violet Lane . . .

Last night Blood's End was quiet; there was some activity in Highland Green; while Dreary Station took the worst of Jerry's effort. And Sidney Slyter has this to say: a beautiful afternoon, a lovely crowd, a taste of bitters, and light returning to the faces of heroic stone—one day there will be amusements everywhere, good fun for our mortality, and you'll whistle and flick your cigarette into an old crater's lip and with your young woman go off to a fancy flutter at the races. For Sidney Slyter was recognized last night. The man was in a litter, an old man propped up in the shelter at Temple Place. I pushed my helmet back and gave him a smoke and all at once he said: "You'll write about the horses again, Sidney! You'll write about the nags again all right. . . ." So keep a lookout for me. Because Sidney Slyter will be looking out for you. . . .

Have you ever let lodgings in the winter? Was there a bed kept waiting, a corner room kept waiting for a gentleman? And have you ever hung a cardboard in the window and, just out of view yourself, watched to see which man would stop and read the hand-lettering on your sign, glance at the premises from roof to little sign —an awkward piece of work—then step up suddenly and hold his finger on your bell? What was it you saw from the window that made you let the bell continue ringing and the bed go empty another night? Something about the eyes? The smooth white skin between the brim of the bowler hat and the eyes?

Or perhaps you yourself were once the lonely lodger. Perhaps you crossed the bridges with the night crowds, listened to the tooting of the river boats and the sounds of shops closing on the far side. Perhaps the moon was behind the cathedral. You walked in the cathedral's shadow while the moon kept shining on three girls ahead. And you followed the moonlit girls. Or followed a woman carrying a market sack, or followed a slow bus high as a house with a saint's stone shadow on its side and smoke coming out from between the tires. Then a turn in the street and broken glass at the foot of a balustrade and you wiped your forehead. And standing still, shoes making idle noise on the smashed glass, you took the packet from inside your coat, unwrapped the oily paper, and far from the tall lamp raised the piece of hot white fish to your teeth.

You must have eaten with your fingers. And you were careful not to lick your lips when you stepped out into the light once more and felt against your face the air waves from the striking of the clock high in the cathedral's stone. The newspaper—it was folded to the listings of single rooms—fell from your coat pocket when you drank from the bottle. But no matter. No need for the rent per week, the names of streets. You were walking now, peering in the windows now, looking for the little signs. How bloody hard it is to read hand-lettering at night. And did your finger ever really touch the bell?

I wouldn't advise Violet Lane—there is no telling about the beds in Violet Lane—but perhaps in Dreary Station you have already found a lodging good as mine, if you were once the gentleman or if you ever took a tea kettle from a lady's hands. A fortnight is all you need. After a fortnight you will set up your burner, prepare hot water for the rubber bottle, warm the bottom of the bed with the bag that leaks round its collar. Or you will turn the table's broken leg to the wall, visit the lavatory in your robe, drive a nail or two with the heel of your boot. After a fortnight they don't evict a man. All those rooms—number twenty-eight, the one the incendiaries burned on Ash Wednesday, the final cubicle that had iron shutters with nymphs and swans and leaves—all those rooms were vacancies in which you started growing fat or first found yourself writing to the lady in the *Post* about salting breast of chicken or sherrying eggs. A lodger is a man who does not forget the cold drafts, the snow on the window ledge, the feel of his knees at night, the taste of a mutton chop in a room in which he held his head all night.

It was from Mother that I learned my cooking.

They were always turning Mother out onto the street. Our pots, our crockery, our undervests, these we kept in cardboard boxes, and from room to empty room we carried them until the strings wore out and her garters and medicines came through the holes. Our boxes lay in spring rains, they gathered snow. Troops, cabmen, bobbies passed them moldering and wet on the street. Once, dried out at last and piled high in a dusty hall, our boxes were set afire. Up narrow stairs and down we carried them, over steps with spikes that caught your boot heels and into small premises still rank with the smells of dead dog or cat. And out of her greasy bodice the old girl paid while I would be off to the unfamiliar lavatory to fetch a pull of tea water in our black pot.

"Here's home, Mother," I would say.

Then down with the skirt, down with the first chemise, off with the little boots. And, hands on the last limp bows: "You may manipulate the screen now, William." It was always behind the boxes, a screen like those standing in theater dressing rooms or in the wards of hospitals, except that it was horsehair brown and filled with holes from her cigarette. And each time we changed our rooms, whether in the morning or midday or dusk, I would set up the screen first thing and behind it Mother would finish stripping to the last scrap of girded rag—the obscene bits of makeshift garb poor old women carry next their skin—and after discarding that would wrap herself in the tawny dressing gown and lie straight upon the single bed while I worked at the burner's pale and rubbery flame. And beyond our door and before the tea was in the cup, we would hear the footsteps, the cheap bracelet tinkling a moment at the glass, would hear the cold fingers lifting down the sign.

Together we took our lodgings, together we went on the street. Fifteen years of circling Dreary Station, she and I, of discovering footprints in the bathtub or a necktie hanging from the toilet chain, or seeing flecks of blood in the shaving glass. Fifteen years with Mother, going from loft to loft in Highland Green, Pinky Road—twice in Violet Lane—and circling all that time the gilded cherubim big as horses that fly off the top of the Dreary Station itself.

If you live long enough with your mother you will learn to cook. Your flesh will know the feel of cabbage leaves, your bare hands will hold everything she eats. Out of the evening paper you will prepare each night your small and tidy wad of cartilage, raw fat, cold and dusty peels and the mouthful—still warm—which she leaves on her plate. And each night as softly as you can, wiping a little blood off the edge of the apron, you will carry your paper bundle down the corridor and into the coldness and falling snow where you will deposit it, soft and square, just under the lid of the landlady's great pail of slops. Mother wipes her lips with your handkerchief and you set the rest of the kidneys on the sooty and frozen window ledge. You cover the burner with its flowered cloth and put the paring knife, the spoon, the end of bread behind the little row of books. There is a place for the pot in the drawer beside the undervests.

In one of the alleys off Pinky Road I remember a little boy who wore black stockings, a shirt ripped off the shoulder, a French sailor's hat with a red pompom. The whipping marks were always fresh on his legs and one cheekbone was blue. A flying goose darkened the mornings in that alley off Pinky Road, the tar buildings were slick with gray goose slime. After the old men and apprentices had left for the high bridges and little shops the place was empty and wet and dead as a lonely dockyard. Then behind the water barrel you could see the boy and his dog.

Each morning when the steam locomotives began shrieking out of Dreary Station the boy knelt on the stones in the leakage from the barrel and caught the puppy by its jowls and rolled its fur and rubbed its ears between his fingers. Alone with the tar doors dripping and the petrol and horse water drifting down the gutters, the boy would waggle the animal's fat head, hide its slow shocked eyes in his hands, flop it upright and listen to its heart. His fingers were always feeling the black gums or the soft wormy little legs or quickly freeing and pulling open the eyes so that he, the thin boy, could stare into them. No fields, sunlight, larks—only the stoned alley like a footpath on a quay down which a black ship might come sailing if the wind held, and down beneath the mists coming off the dead steeplecocks the boy with the poor dog in his arms and loving his close scrutiny of the nicks in its ears, tiny channels over the dog's brain, pictures he could find on its purple tongue, pearls he could discover between the claws. Love is a long close scrutiny like that. I loved Mother in the same way.

I see her: it is just before the end; she is old; I see her through the red light of my glass of port. See the yellow hair, the eyes drying up in the corners. She laughs and jerks her head but the mouth is open, and that is what I see through the glass of port: the laughing lips drawn round a stopper of darkness and under the little wax chin a great silver fork with a slice of bleeding meat that rises slowly, slowly, over the dead dimple in the wax, past the sweat under the first lip, up to the level of her eyes so she can take a look at it before she eats. And I wait for the old girl to choke it down.

But there is a room waiting if you can find it, there is a joke somewhere if you can bring it to your lips. And my landlord, Mr. Banks, is not the sort to evict a man for saying a kind word to his wife or staying in the parlor past ten o'clock. His wife, Margaret, says I was a devoted son.

Yes, devoted. I remember fifteen years of sleeping, fifteen years of smelling cold shoes in the middle of the night and waiting, wondering whether I smelled smoke down the hallway to the toilet or smelled smoke coming from the parlor that would burn like hay. I think of the whipped boy and his dog abed with him and that's what devotion is: sleeping with a wet dog beneath your pillow or humming some childish tune to your mother the whole night through while waiting for the plaster, the beams, the glass, the kidneys on the sill to catch fire. Margaret's estimation of my character is correct. Heavy men are most often affectionate. And I, William Hencher, was a large man even then.

"Don't worry about it, Hencher," the captain said. "We'll carry you out if we have to." On its cord the bulb was circling round his head, and across the taverns and walls and craters of Dreary Station came the sirens and engines of the night. Sometimes, at the height of it, the captain and his man—an ex-corporal with rotten legs who wore a red beret and was given to fainting in the hall—went out to walk in the streets, and I would watch them go and wait, watch the searchlights fix upon the wounded cherubim like giants caught naked in the sky, until I heard them swearing in the hall again and, from the top of the stair, an unfamiliar voice crying, "Shut the door. Oh, for the love of bleeding Hell, come shut the door."

We were so close to the old malevolent station that I could hear the shifting of the sandbags piled round it and could hear the locomotives shattering into bits of iron. And one night wouldn't a cherubim's hand or arm or curly head come flying down through our roof? Some dislodged ball of saintly brass palm or muscle or jagged neck find its target in Lily Eastchip's house? But I wasn't destined to die with a fat brass finger in my belly.

To think that Mr. and Mrs. Banks—Michael and Margaret—were only children then, as small and crouching and black-eyed as the boy with the French sailor's hat and the dog. It is a pity I did not know them then: somehow I would have cared for them.

Such things don't want forgetting. When they anchored

a barrage balloon over number twenty-eight—how long it was since we had been evicted from that room—and when the loft in Highland Green had burned Ash Wednesday, and during those days when the water would curl a horse's lip and somebody's copy of *The Vicar of Wakefield* was run over by a fire truck outside my door, why then there was plenty of soot and scum the memory could not let go of.

There was Lily Eastchip with bird feathers round her throat and a dusty rag up the tiny pearl lacing of her sleeve; there was the captain dishonorably mustered from the forces; there was the front of our narrow lodging which the firemen kept hosing down for luck; there was the pink slipper left caught by its heel in the stairway rungs and hanging toe first into the dark of that dry plaster hall. And there were our boxes with broken strings, piled in the hallway and rising toward the slipper, all the cartons I had not the heart to drag to Mother's room. So I see the pasty corporal—Sparrow was his name—rubbing together the handles of his canes, I see Miss Eastchip serving soup, I see Mother's dead livid face. And I shall always see the bomber with its bulbous front gunner's nest flattened over the cistern in the laundry court.

Margaret remembers none of it and Mr. Banks, her husband, is not a talker. But Miss Eastchip's brother went down in his spotter's steeple, tin hat packed red with embers and both feet in the enormous boots burning with a gas-blue flame. Lily got word of it the eve he fell and with the duster hanging down her wrist and the tears on her cheek she looked as if someone had touched a candle to her nightdress in the dark of our teatime. She stood behind the captain's chair whispering, "That's the end for me, the end for me," while the bearer of the news merely sat for a moment, teacup rattling in the saucer and helmet gripped between his knees.

"Well, sorry to bring distressing information," the warden had said. "You'd better keep the curtains on good tonight. We're in for it, I'm afraid."

A pale snow was coming down when he passed my window—a black square-shouldered man—and I saw the dark shape of him and the gleam off the silvery whistle caught in his teeth. Somebody laid the cold table, and far-off we heard the first dull boom and breath, as if they had blown out a candle as tall as St. George's spire.

"Good night, Hencher. . . ."

"Good night, Captain. Mother gave you the salts for Lily, did she?"

"She did. And—Hencher—if anything uncommon occurs in the night, you can always give me a signal on the pipes."

"I'll just do that, Captain. It's good of you."

Mother got the covers to her chin and, lights off, blackout drawn aside, I sat watching to see the aircraft shoot out the eyes of the cherubim who, beyond sifting snow, and triangulated, now and then, by flooding white shafts of light, hugged each other atop the Dreary Station dome. I held my cheeks. I listened to the old girl's chamber pot—she had stuffed it with jewelry and glass buttons and an ostrich plume—that rolled about beneath the bed. Missing one front wheel, a tiny tar-painted lorry passed in dreadful crawl and the bare hub of its broken axle screeched and sent off sparks against the stones. And all through that blistering snowy night my hands were drenching the angora white yarn of a tasseled shawl, twisting it like a young girl's lock of hair.

When engines shook the night beyond the nymphs and apple leaves in the filigreed shutters of my window, I began suddenly to smell it: not the stench of rafters burning, not the vaporized rubber stench that stayed about the street for days after the hit on the garage of Autorank, Limited, but only a faint live smell of worn carpet or paper or tissue being singed within the lodging house itself. And I fancied it was coming round the edges of my door—the odor of smoke—and I held to the arms of my chair and slowly breathed into my lungs that smoke.

"Are you awake?" I said.

She sat up with the nightdress slanting down her flesh.

"You'd better put your wrapper on, old girl."

She sat there startled by the light of a flare that was plainly going to land in old John's chimney across the way. I could see her game face and I squeezed on the slippers and squeezed the shawl.

"Don't you smell the smoke? The house is going up," I said. "Do you want to burn?"

"It's only the kettle, William. . . ." And she was grinning, one foot was trying to escape the sheet. They were running with buckets across the way at John's.

"You look, William, you tell me what it is. . . ."

"Out of that bed now, and we'll just have a look together."

Then I pulled open the door and there was the hallway dry and dark as ever, the slipper still hooked on the stair, the one faint bulb swinging round and round on its cord. But our boxes were burning. The bottom of the pile was sunk in flame, hot crabbing flame orange and pale blue in the draft from the door and the sleeve of a coat of mine was crumbling and smoking out of a black pasty hole.

Mother began to cough and pull at my hand—the smoke was mostly hers and thick, and there is no smudge as black as that from burning velveteen and stays and packets of cheap face powder—and then she cried, "Oh, William, William." I saw the pile lean and dislodge a clump of cinders while at the same moment I heard a warden tapping on the outside door with his torch and heard him call through the door: "All right in there?"

I could taste my portion of the smoke; the banging on the door grew louder. Now they were flinging water on old John's roof, but mother and I were in an empty hall with only our own fire to care about.

"Can't you leave off tugging on me, can't you?" But before I could close my robe she was gone, three or four steps straight into the pile to snatch the stays and an old tortoise-shell fan from out of the fire.

"Mum!"

But she pulled, the boxes toppled about her, the flames shot high as the ceiling. While a pink flask of ammonia she had saved for years exploded and hissed with the rest of it.

From under the pall I heard her voice: "Look here, it's hardly singed at all, see now? Hardly singed . . ." Outside footfalls, and then the warden: "Charlie, you'd better give us a hand here, Charlie. . . ."

On hands and knees she was trying to crawl back to me, hot sparks from the fire kept settling on her arms and on the thin silk of her gown. One strap was burned through suddenly, fell away, and then a handful of tissue in the bosom caught and, secured by the edging of charred lace, puffed at its luminous peak as if a small forced fire, stoked inside her flesh, had burst a hole through the tender dry surface of my mother's breast.

"Give us your shoulder here, Charlie . . . lend a heave!"

And even while I grunted and went at her with robe outspread, she tried with one hand to pluck away her bosom's fire. "Mother," I shouted, "hold on now, Mother," and knelt and got the robe round her—mother and son in a single robe—and was slapping the embers and lifting her back toward the bed when I saw the warden's boot in the door and heard the tooting of his whistle. Then only the sound of dumping sand, water falling, and every few minutes the hurried crash of an ax head into our smothered pile.

At dawn I returned to the charcoal of the hall and met the captain in corduroy jacket and wearing a gun and holster next his ribs. For a moment we stood looking at the scorch marks on the lath and the high black reach of extinguished flames. The captain ran his toe through the ashes.

"How is your mother, Hencher? A bit hard on her, wasn't it?"

"She won't say, of course, though the pain must be considerable. . . ."

"Well, Hencher," rattling tin and glass in his pocket, "give me a call on the pipes if it gets worse. I happen to have a needle and a few drops in an ampule can relieve all that."

"Oh, she'll do quite nicely, I'm sure. . . ."

But the blisters did not go down. They were small, translucent, membranous and tough all over her body, and no matter how often I dressed them with marge from Lily's kitchen they retained their bulbous density. And even today I smell them: smell the skin, smell the damp sheets I wrapped her in, smell that room turned infirmary. I smell that house.

For after a decade it is the same house, a different landlord—Michael Banks now, not poor grieving Lily—but the same house, the one in the middle of Corking Street not five minutes east of the station. Refurbished, an electric buzzer at the door, three flats instead of beds for lodgers, and a spirit shop where John's house stood—from the peaked garret to the electric buzzer it is the exact same place. I know it well. A lodger is forever going back to the pictures in black bead frames, back to the lost slipper, or forever coming round to pay respects when you think you've seen the last of him, or to tell you—stranger as far as you know—that his was the cheek that left the bloody impression in your looking glass. "My old girl died on these premises, Mr. Banks," looking over his shoulder, feeling the wall, and he had to take me in. And then it was home again for William when I found the comforter with hearts on it across my bed. Now there are orange deck chairs in the laundry court, and sitting out with a sack of beans on my stomach and hearing the sounds of the wireless from Annie's window, still through half-shut eyes I see the shadow of the bomber that once filled the court.

Sometimes I wake in the night, very late in the still night, and go sit in the lavatory and run the water and smoke half a thin cigar until there is nothing to feel, nothing to hear except Margaret turning over or the cat pacing my step in the parlor. I see the cherubim safely lit, I wipe my hands, I sleep.

I waited three weeks before signaling the captain on the pipes, and then I beat at them with my slipper until I threw it across the room and found the warden's torch in the covers and, after the blow that smashed the glass, fetched the captain with loud strokes on first the hot water pipe and then the cold. Together they came, captain and corporal, while the pipes still shivered up the wall. I looked away when I saw the captain pulling out the plunger.

"You ain't going to give my stuff to her?" said Sparrow. "Not to the old woman, are you? I'd sooner you give a jab to this fat man here. . . ."

I trembled then.

"No use giving my stuff to her," said Sparrow, the corporal.

And then in the dark: "She'll do now, Hencher. I'd get a little sleep if I were you."

But it was not sleep I wanted. I fastened the robe, tied the white shawl round my throat. "Good night, old girl," I whispered and went out of the door, flinging an end of the shawl aside flier fashion. It was cold; I walked beneath the black supports and timbers of a burned city, and how often I had made passage through the length of Lily Eastchip's corridor, carried my neat square of dinner garbage past the parlor when Mother and I first joined that household and ate alone. No garbage now. Only the parlor with pinholes in the curtain across the window and a pile of clothing and several candles in the fireplace; only the hallway growing more and more narrow at the end; only the thought that, behind the screen, I had left Mother comfortable and that tonight, this night, I was going to stand bareheaded in the laundry court and breathe, watch the sky, hear what I could of the cries coming from Violet Lane, from the oil-company docks, the Mall. When I found the bolt and pulled it, squeezed out of that black entrance with a hand to my throat, I expected to see the boy dancing with his dog.

The light snow fell, tracers went straight up from behind the garret that faced me across the court, I noticed a pink reflection in the sky west of the station. The airplanes were bombing Highland Green. I saw the humps of dead geraniums and a wooden case of old stout bottles black and glistening against a shed. I had not moved, I felt the snow wet on my shoulders and on the rims of my ears.

Large, brown, a lifeless airplane returning, it was one of our own and I saw it suddenly approach out of the snow perhaps a hundred feet above the garret and slow as a child's kite. Big and blackish-brown with streaks of ice across the nose, which was beginning to rise while the tail sank behind in the snow, it was simply there, enormous and without a trace of smoke, the engines dead and one aileron flapping in the wind. And ceasing to climb, ceasing to move, a vast and ugly shape stalled against the snow up there, the nose dropped and beneath the pilot's window I saw the figure of a naked woman painted against the bomber's pebbly surface. Her face was snow, something back of her thigh had sprung a leak and the thigh was sunk in oil. But her hair, her long white head of hair was shrieking in the wind as if the inboard engine was sucking the strands of it.

Her name was Reggie's Rose and she was sitting on the black pack of a parachute.

Dipped, shuddered, banged up and down for a moment—I could see the lifted rudder then, swinging to and fro above the tubular narrowing of its fuselage—and during that slapping glide the thick wings did not fall, no frenzied hand wiped the pilot's icy windscreen, no tiny torch switched on to prove this final and outrageous landfall. It made no sound, but steepened its glide, then slowed again with a kind of gigantic deranged and stubborn confidence and pushed on, shedding the snow, as if after the tedium of journey there would be a mere settling, rolling to silence, with a drink and hot sandwiches for her crew. And I myself fell down next to Lily Eastchip's garbage tin, in darkness drove my cheek among the roots of her dead bushes. Through the dressing robe and bedroom silks the heat of my body dissolved the snow. I was wet and waited for the blow of a flying gyroscopic compass or propeller blade.

Or to be brushed to death by a wing, caught beneath cold tons of the central fuselage, or surely sprayed by petrol and burned alive: tasting those hard white rubber roots I wondered whether the warden and his friend Charlie would hear the crash. And tightening, biting to the sour heart of the root, I saw the bomber in its first shapeless immensity and thought I could hold it off—monstrous, spread-winged, shadowy—hold it off with my outstretched arms eternally or at least until I should escape by Lily's door.

The warden must have heard the crash. His Charlie must have heard the crash.

Something small and round struck suddenly against my side. When again I made out the sounds from the far corner—the steady firing of the guns—I breathed, rolled, sat with my back to the wall. My fingers found the painful missile, only a hard tuft of wool blown loose from inside a pilot's boot or torn from the shaggy collar of his flying coat. The snow was falling, still the sky was pink from the bombing of Highland Green. But no whistles, no wardens running: a single window smashed on the other side of the court and a woman began shrieking for her husband. And again there was only silence and my belly trembling.

I took one step, another. Then there were the high dark sides of the intact bomber and the snow was melting on the iron. I reached the first three-bladed propeller —the two bottom sweeps of steel were doubled beneath the cowling—and for a moment I leaned against it and it was like touching your red cheek to a stranded whale's fluke when, in all your coastal graveyard, there was no witness, no one to see. I walked round the bubble of the nose—that small dome set on edge with a great crack down the middle—and stood beneath the artistry of Reggie's Rose. Her leg was long, she sat on her parachute with one knee raised. In the knee cap was a half-moon hole for a man's boot, above it another, and then a hand grip just under the pilot's door. So I climbed up poor Rose, the airman's dream and big as one of the cherubim, and snatched at the high door which, sealed in the flight's vacuum, sucked against its fitting of rust and rubber and sprang open.

I should have had a visored cap, leather coat, gauntlets. But, glancing once at the ground, poised in the snow over Rose's hair, I tugged, entered head first the forward cabin.

The cabin roof as well as the front gunner's dome was cracked and a little snow fell steadily between the seats. In the dark I sat with my hands on the half wheel and slippers resting on the jammed pedals, my head turning to see the handles, rows of knobs, dials with needles all set at zero, boxes and buttons and toggle switches and loop of wire and insulated rings coming down from the roof. In this space I smelled resin and grease and lacquer and something fatty that made me groan.

I tried to work the pedals, turn the wheel. I could not breathe. When suddenly from a hook between two cylinders next to my right hand I saw a palm-shaped cone of steel and took it up, held it before my face—a metal kidney trimmed round the edges with a strip of fur—I looked at it, then lowered my head and pressed my nose and mouth into its drawn cup. My breath came free. The inhalation was pure and deep and sweet. I smelled tobacco and a cheap wine, was breathing out of the pilot's lungs.

Cold up here. Cold up here. Give a kiss to Rose.

Surely it was Reggie's breath—the tobacco he had got in an Egyptian NAAFI, his cheap wine—frozen on the slanting translucent glass of the forward cabin's windows. Layer overlapping icy layer of Reggie's breath. And I clapped the mask back on its hook, turned a wheel on the cylinder. Leaning far over, sweating, I thrust my hands down and pushed them back along the aluminum trough of floor and found the bottle. Then I found something else, something cool and round to the skin, something that had rested there behind my heels all this while. I set the bottle on top of the wireless box—I heard the sounds of some strange brass anthem coming from the earphones—and reached for that black round shape, carefully and painfully lifted it and cradled it in my lap.

The top of the flying helmet was a perfect dome. Hard, black, slippery. And the flaps were large. On the surface all the leather of that helmet was soft—if you rubbed it—and yet bone hard and firm beneath the hand's polishing. There were holes for wire plugs, bands for the elastic of a pair of goggles, some sort of worn insignia on the front. A heavy wet leather helmet large enough for me. I ran my fingernail across the insignia, picked at a blemish, and suddenly I leaned forward, turned the helmet over, looked inside. Then I lifted the helmet, gripped it steadily at arm's length—I was sitting upright now, upright and staring at the polished thing I held—and slowly raised it high and twisting it, hitching it down from side to side, settled the helmet securely on my own smooth head. I extended my hands again and took the wheel.

"How's the fit, old girl?" I whispered. "A pretty good fit, old girl?" And I turned my head as far to the right as I was able, so that she might see how I—William Hencher—looked with my bloody coronet in place at last.

Give a kiss to Rose.

Between 3 and 4 A.M. on the night she died—so many years ago—that's when I set out walking with my great black coat that made the small children laugh, walking alone or sometimes joining the crowds and waiting under the echoes of the dome and amid the girders and shattered skylight of Dreary Station to see another trainload of our troops return. So many years ago. And I had my dreams; I had my years of walking to the cathedral in the moonlight.

"My old girl died on these premises, Mr. Banks."

And then all the years were gone and I recognized that house, that hall, despite the paint and plaster and the cheap red carpet they had tacked on the parlor floor. I paid him in advance, I did, and he put the money in his trouser pocket while Margaret went to lift their awkward sign out of the window. Fresh paint, fresh window glass, new floorboards here and there: to think of the place not gutted after all but still standing, the house lived in now by those with hardly a recollection of the nightly fires. Cheery, new, her dresses in one of the closets and his hat by the door. But one of his four rooms was mine, surely mine, and I knew I'd smell the old dead odor of smoke if only I pushed my face close enough to those shabby walls.

Here's home, old girl, here's home.

So I spent my first long night in the renovated room, and I dared not spend that night in the lavatory but smoked my cigars in bed. Sitting up in bed, smoking, thinking of my mother all night long. And then there was the second night and I ventured into the hallway. There was the third night and in the darkened cubicle I listened to the far bells counting two, three, four o'clock in the morning and all that time—thinking now of comfort, tranquillity, and thinking also of their two clasped hands—I wondered what I might do for them. The bells were slow in counting, the water dripped. And suddenly it was quite clear what I could do for them, for Michael and his wife.

I hooked the lavatory door. Then I filled the porcelain sink, and in darkness smelling of lavender and greasy razor blades I immersed my hands up to the wrists, soaked them silently. I dried them on a stiff towel, pushing the towel between my fingers again and again. I wiped the top of my head until it burned. Then I used his talc, showed my teeth in the glass, straightened the robe. I took up the pink-shelled hair brush for a moment but replaced it. And off to the kitchen and then on boards that made tiny sounds, walking with a heavy man's sore steps, noticing a single lighted window across the court.

It grew cold and before dawn I left the kitchen once: only to pull the comforter off my bed. Again in the kitchen and on Margaret's wooden stool I sat with the comforter hooded round my head and shoulders, sat waiting for the dawn to come fishing up across the chimney pots and across that dirty gable in the apex of which a weathered muse's face was carved. When I heard the dog barking in the flat upstairs, when water started running in the pipes behind the wall, and a few river gulls with icy feathers hovered outside the window, and light from a sun the color of some guardsman's breast warmed my hooded head and arms and knees—why then I got off the stool, began to move about. Wine for the eggs, two pieces of buttered toast, two fried strips of mackerel, a teapot small as an infant's head and made of iron and boiling—it was a tasteful tray, in one corner decorated with a few pinched violet buds I tore from the plant that has always grown on Margaret's window shelf. I looked round, made certain the jets were off, thought to include a saucer of red jam, covered the hot salted portions with folded table napkins. Then I listened. I heard nothing but the iron clock beating next to the stove and a boot landing near the dog upstairs.

The door was off the latch and they were sleeping. I turned and touched it with my hip, my elbow, touched it with only a murmur. And it swung away on smooth hinges while I watched and listened until it came up sharply against the corner of a little cane chair. They lay beneath a single sheet and a single sand-colored blanket, and I saw that on his thin icy cheeks Banks had grown a beard in the night and that Margaret—the eyelids defined the eyes, her lips were dry and brown and puffy—had been dreaming of a nice picnic in narrow St. George's Park behind the station. Behind each silent face was the dream that would collect slack shadows and tissues and muscles into some first mood for the day. Could I not blow smiles onto their nameless lips, could I not force apart those lips with kissing? One of the gulls came round from the kitchen and started beating the glass.

"Here's breakfast," I said, and pushed my knees against the footboard.

For a moment the vague restless dreams merely went faster beneath those two faces. Then stopped suddenly, quite fixed in pain. Then both at once they opened their eyes and Banks' were opalescent, quick, the eyes of a boy, and Margaret's eyes were brown.

"It's five and twenty past six," I said. "Take the tray now, one of you. Tea's getting cold. . . ."

Banks sat up and smiled. He was wearing an undervest, his arms were naked and he stretched them toward me. "You're not a bad sort, Hencher," he said. "Give us the tray!"

"Oh, Mr. Hencher," I heard the warm voice, the slow sounds in her mouth, "you shouldn't have gone to the trouble. . . ."

It was a small trouble. And not long after—a month or a fortnight perhaps—I urged them to take a picnic, not to the sooty park behind the station but farther away, farther away to Landingfield Battery, where they could sit under a dead tree and hold their poor hands. And while they were gone I prowled through the flat, softened my heart of introspection: I found her small tube of cosmetic for the lips and, in the lavatory, drew a red circle with it round each of my eyes. I had their bed to myself while they were gone. They came home laughing and brought a postal card of an old pocked cannon for me.

It was the devil getting the lipstick off.

But red circles, giving your landlord's bed a try, keeping his flat to yourself for a day—a man must take possession of a place if it is to be a home for the waiting out of dreams. So we lead our lives, keep our privacy in Dreary Station, spend our days grubbing at the rubber roots, pausing at each other's doors. I still fix them breakfast now and again and the cherubim are still my monument. I have my billet, my memories. How permanent some transients are at last. In a stall in Dreary Station there is a fellow with vocal cords damaged during the fire who sells me chocolates, and I like to talk to him; sometimes I come across a gagger lying out cold in the snow, and for him I have a word; I like to talk to all the unanswering children of Dreary Station. But home is best.

I hear Michael in the bath, I whet Margaret's knives. Or it is 3 or 4 A.M. and I turn the key, turn the knob, avoid the empty goldfish bowl that catches the glitter off the street, feel the skin of my shoes going down the hallway to their door. I stand whispering our history before that door and slowly, so slowly, I step behind the screen in my own dark room and then, on the edge of the bed and sighing, start peeling the elastic sleeves off my thighs. I hold my head awhile and then I rub my thighs until the sleep goes out of them and the blood returns. In my own dark room I hear a little bird trying to sing on the ledge where the kidneys used to freeze.

Smooth the pillow, pull down the sheets for me. Thinking of Reggie and the rest of them, can I help but smile?

I can get along without you, Mother.

1

SIDNEY SLYTER SAYS

Happy Throngs Arrive at Aldington for Golden Bowl . . .

Mystery Horse to Run in Classic Race . . .

Rock Castle: Dark Horse or Foul Play?

Gray toppers, gray gloves and polished walking sticks; elegant ladies and smart young girls; fellows in fedoras, and mothers, and wives—all your Cheapside crowd along with your own Sidney Slyter, naturally. Pure life is the only phrase that will do, life's pure anticipation. . . . So you won't want to show up here without a flower in your buttonhole, I can tell you that. . . . The horses are lovely. Sidney Slyter's choice? Marlowe's Pippet without a doubt—to win (I took a few pints last night with a young woman, a delightful Mrs. Sybilline Laval, who said that Candy Stripe looked very good. But you'll agree with Slyter. He knows his horses, eh?) . . . A puzzling late entry is Rock Castle, owned by one Mr. Michael Banks. But more of this . . .

It is Wednesday dawn. Margaret's day, once every fortnight, for shopping and looking in the windows. She is off already with mints in her pocket and a great empty crocheted bag on her arm, jacket pulled down nicely on her hips and a fresh tape on her injured finger. She smells of rose water and the dust that is always gathering in the four rooms. In one of the shops she will hold a plain dress against the length of her body, then return it to the racks; at a stand near the bridge she will buy him—Michael Banks—a tin of fifty, and for Hencher she will buy three cigars. She will ride the double-decker, look at dolls behind a glass, have a sandwich. And come home at last with a packet of cold fish in the bag.

Most Wednesdays—let her stay, let her walk out—Michael does not care, does not hold his breath, never listens for the soft voice that calls good-by. But this is no usual Wednesday dawn and he slips from room to room until she is finally gone. In front of the glass fixes his coat and hat, and smiles. For he intends not to be home when she returns.

Now he is standing next to their bed—the bed of ordinary down and ticking and body scent, with the course of dreams mapped on the coverlet—and not beside the door and not in the hall. Ready for street, departure, for some prearranged activity, he nonetheless is immobile this moment and stares at the bed. His gold tooth is warm in the sun, his rotting tooth begins to pain. From out the window the darting of a black tiny bird makes him wish for its sound. He would like to hear it or would like to hear sounds of a wireless through the open door or sounds of tugs and double-deckers and boys crying the news. Perhaps the smashing of a piece of furniture. Anything. Because he too has his day to discover and it is more than pretty dresses and gandering at a shiny steam iron and taking a quick cup of tea.

He can tell the world.

But in the silence of the flat's close and ordinary little bedroom he hears again all the soft timid sounds she made before setting off to market: the fall of the slippery soap bar into the empty tub, the limpid sound of her running bath, the slough of three fingers in the cream pot, the cry of bristles against her teeth, the fuzzy sound of straps drawing up on the skin of her shoulders; poor sounds of her counting out the change, click of the pocketbook. Then sounds of a safety pin closing beneath the lifted skirt and of the comb setting up last-minute static in the single wave of her hair.

He pulls at the clothes-closet door. He steps inside and embraces two hanging and scratchy dresses and her winter coat pinned over with bits of tissue. Something on a hook knocks his hat awry. Behind him, in the room, the sunlight has burned past the chimes in St. George's belfry and is now more than a searching shaft in that room: it comes diffused and hot through the window glass, it lights the dry putty-colored walls and ceiling, draws a steam from the damp lath behind the plaster, warms the small unpainted tin clock which she always leaves secreted and ticking under the pillow on her side of the bed. A good early-morning sun, good for the cat or for the humming housewife. But the cat is in the other room and his wife is out.

Inside the closet he is rummaging overhead to a shelf —reaching and pushing among the dresses now, invading anew and for himself this hiding place which he expects to keep from her. He stands on tiptoe, an arm is angular at the crook, his unused hand is dragging one of the dresses off its hanger by the shoulder; but the other set of high fingers is pushing, working a way through the dusty folds toward what he knows is resting behind the duster and pail near the wall. His hipbone strikes the thin paneling of the door so that it squeaks and swings outward, casting a perfect black shadow across the foot of the bed. And after a moment he steps out into the room, turns sideways, uncorks the bottle, tilts it up, and puts the hot mouth of the bottle to his lips. He drinks— until the queer mechanism of his throat can pass no more and his lips stop sucking and a little of it spills down his chin. Upstairs a breakfast kettle begins to shriek. He takes a step, holds the bottle against his breast, suddenly turns his face straight to the sun.

She'll wonder about me. She'll wonder where her hubby's at, rightly enough.

He left the flat door open. Throughout the day, whenever anyone moved inside the building, slammed a window or shouted a few words down the unlighted stair— "Why don't you leave off it? Why don't you just leave off it, you with your bloody kissing round the gas works"—the open door swung a hand's length to and fro, drifted its desolate and careless small arc in a house of shadow and brief argument. But no one took notice of the door, no one entered the four empty rooms beyond it, and only the abandoned cat followed with its turning head each swing of the door. Until at the end of the day Margaret came in smiling, walked the length of the hall with a felt hat over one ear, feet hot, market sack pulling from the straps in her hand and, stopping short, discovered the waiting animal in the door's crack. Stopped, backed off, went for help from a second-floor neighbor who had a heart large with comfort and all the cheer in the world, went for help as he knew she would.

Knowing how much she feared his dreams: knowing that her own worst dream was one day to find him gone, overdue minute by minute some late afternoon until the inexplicable absence of him became a certainty; knowing that his own worst dream, and best, was of a horse which was itself the flesh of all violent dreams; knowing this dream, that the horse was in their sitting room—he had left the flat door open as if he meant to return in a moment or meant never to return—seeing the room empty except for moonlight bright as day and, in the middle of the floor, the tall upright shape of the horse draped from head to tail in an enormous sheet that falls over the eyes and hangs down stiffly from the silver jaw; knowing the horse on sight and listening while it raises one shadowed hoof on the end of a silver thread of foreleg and drives down the hoof to splinter in a single crash one plank of that empty Dreary Station floor; knowing his own impurity and Hencher's guile; and knowing that Margaret's hand has nothing in the palm but a short life span (finding one of her hairpins in his pocket that Wednesday dawn when he walked out into the sunlight with nothing cupped in the lip of his knowledge except thoughts of the night and pleasure he was about to find) —knowing all this, he heard in Hencher's first question the sound of a dirty wind, a secret thought, the sudden crashing in of the plank and the crashing shut of that door.

"How's the missus, Mr. Banks? Got off to her marketing all right?"

Then: "No offense. No offense," said Hencher after Banks' pause and answer.

The *Artemis*—a small excursion boat—shivered and rolled now and again ever so slightly though it was moored fast to the quay. Banks heard the cries of dock hands who were fixing a boom's hook to a cargo net, the sound of a pump, and the sound, from the top deck, of a child shouting through cupped hands in the direction of the river's distant traffic of puffing tugs and barges. And also overhead there were the quick uncontrollable running footfalls of smaller children and, on the gangway, hidden beyond the white bulkhead of the refreshment saloon, there was the steady tramp of still more boarding passengers.

A bar, a dance floor—everyone was dancing—a row of salt-sealed windows, a small skylight drawn over with the shadow of a fat gull: here was Hencher's fun, and Banks could feel the crowd mounting the sides of the ship, feel the dance rhythm tingling through the greasy wood of the table top beneath his hand. For a moment and in a clear space past the open sea doors held back by small brass hooks, he saw hatless members of the crew dragging a mountain of battered life preservers forward in a great tar-stained shroud of canvas.

"No offense, eh, Mr. Banks? Too good a day for that. And tell me now, how's this for a bit of a good trip?"

The lodger's hand was putty round the bottom of the beer glass, the black-and-cream checkered cap was tight on the head—surely the fat man would sail away with the mothers and children and smart young girls when the whistle blew.

"No offense, Hencher. But you can leave off mentioning her, if you don't mind."

Perhaps he would sail away himself. That would be the laugh, he and Hencher, stowaways both, elbowing room at the ship's rail between lovers and old ladies, looking out themselves—the two of them—for a glimpse of the water or a great furnace burning far-off at the river's edge. Sail away out of the river's mouth and into the afternoons of an excursion life. Hear the laughter, feel the ship's beam wallow in the deep seas and lie down at night beneath a lifeboat's white spongy prow still hot to the hand. No luggage, no destination, helmsman tying the wheel—on any course—to have a smoke with a girl. This would be the laugh, with only the pimply barkeep who had never been to sea before drawing beer the night long. But there was better than this in wait for him, something much better than this.

In the crowd at the foot of the gangplank an officer had asked for their tickets, and Hencher had spoken to the man: "My old woman's on that boat, Captain, and me and my friend here will just see that she's got a proper deck chair and a robe round her legs."

And now the dawn was gone, the morning hours too were gone. He had found the crabbed address and come upon the doorway in which Hencher waited; had walked with him down all those streets until the squat ship, unseaworthy, just for pleasure, lay ahead of them in a berth between two tankers; had already seen the rigging, the smokestacks, the flesh-colored masts and rusty sirens and whistles in a blue sky above the rotting roof of the cargo sheds; had boarded the *Artemis*, which smelled of coke and rank canvas and sea animals and beer and boys looking for sport.

"We'll just have some drink and a little talk on this ship before she sails, Mr. Banks. . . ."

He leaned toward Hencher. His elbows were on the table and his wet glass was touching Hencher's frothy glass in the center of the table. Someone had dropped a mustard pot and beneath his shoe he felt the fragments of smashed china, the shape of a wooden spoon, the slick of the mustard on the dirty spoon. A woman with lunch packed in a box pushed through the crowd and bumped against him, paused and rested the box upon their table. Protruding from the top of the box and sealed with a string and paper was a tall jar filled with black bottled tea. The woman carried her own folding chair.

"Bloody slow in putting to sea, mates," she said, and laughed. She wore an old sweater, a man's muffler was knotted round her throat. "I could do with a breath of that sea air right now, I could."

Hencher lifted his glass. "Go on," he said, "have a sip. Been on the *Artemis* before?"

"Not me."

"I'll tell you then. Find a place for yourself in the bows. You get the breeze there, you see everything best from there."

She put her mouth to the foam, drank long, and when she took the glass away she was breathing quickly and a canker at the edge of her lip was wet. "Join me," she said. "Why don't you join me, mates?"

"We'll see you in the bows," said Hencher.

"Really?"

"Good as my word."

It was all noise of people wanting a look at the world and a smell of the sea, and the woman was midships with her basket; soon in the shadow of the bow anchor she would be trying to find a safe spot for her folding chair. Hencher was winking. A boy in a black suit danced by their table, and in his arms was a girl of about fourteen. Banks watched the way she held him and watched her hands in the white gloves shrunk small and tight below the girl's thin wrists. Music, laughter, smells of deck paint and tide and mustard, sight of the boy pulled along by the fierce white childish hands. And he himself was listening, touching his tongue to the beer, leaning close as he dared to Hencher, beginning to think of the black water widening between the sides of the holiday ship and the quay.

"What's that, Hencher? What's that you say?"

Hencher was looking him full in the face: ". . . to Rock Castle, here's to Rock Castle, Mr. Banks!"

He heard his own voice beneath the whistles and plash of bilge coming out of a pipe, "To Rock Castle, then. . . ."

The glasses touched, were empty, and the girl's leg was only the leg of a child and the woman would drink her black tea alone. He stood, moved his chair so that he sat not across from Hencher but beside him.

"He's old, Mr. Banks. Rock Castle has his age, he has. And what's his age? Why, it's the evolution of his bloody name, that's what it is. Just the evolution of a name—Apprentice out of Lithograph by Cobbler, Emperor's Hand by Apprentice out of Hand Maiden by Lord of the Land, Draftsman by Emperor's Hand out of Shallow Draft by Amulet, Castle Churl by Draftsman out of Likely Castle by Cold Masonry, Rock Castle by Castle Churl out of Words on Rock by Plebeian—and what's this name if not the very evolution of his life? You want to think of the life, Mr. Banks, think of the breeding. Consider the fiver bets, the cheers, the wreaths. Then forgotten, because he's taken off the turf and turned out into the gorse, far from the paddock, the swirl of torn ticket stubs, the soothing nights after a good win, far from the serpentine eyes and bowler hats. Do you see it, Mr. Banks? Do you see how it was for Rock Castle?"

He could only nod, but once again—the *Artemis* was rolling—once again he saw the silver jaw, the enormous sheet, the upright body of the horse that was crashing in the floor of the Dreary Station flat. And he could only keep his eyes down, clasp his hands.

". . . Back sways a little, you see, the color of the coat hardens and the legs grow stiff. Months, years, it's only the blue sky for him, occasionally put to stud and then back he goes to his shelter under an old oak at the edge of a field. Useless, you see. Do you see it? Until tonight when he's ours—yours—until tonight when we get our hands on him and tie him up in the van and drive him to stables I know of in Highland Green. Yours, you see, and he's got no recollection of the wreaths or seconds of speed, no knowledge at all of the prime younger horses sprung from his blood. But he'll run all right, on a long track he'll run better than the young ones good for nothing except a sprint. Power, endurance, a forgotten name—do you see it, Mr. Banks? He's ancient, Rock Castle is, an ancient horse and he's bloody well run beyond memory itself. . . ."

Flimsy frocks, dancing children, a boy with the face of a man, a girl whose body was still awkward; they were all about him and taking their pleasure while the feet tramped and the whistle tooted. But Hencher was talking, holding him by the brown coat just beneath the ribs, then fumbling and cupping in front of his eyes a tiny photograph and saying, "Go on, go on, take a gander at this lovely horse."

Then the pause, the voice less friendly and the question, and the sound of his own voice answering: "I'm game, Hencher. Naturally, I'm still game. . . ."

"Ah, like me you are. Good as your word. Well, come then, let's have a turn round the deck of this little tub. We've time yet for a turn at the rail."

He stood, trying to scrape the shards of the smashed mustard pot from his shoe, followed Hencher toward the white sea doors. The back of Hencher's neck was red, the checked cap was at an angle, they made their slow way together through the excursion crowd and the smells of soap and cotton underwear and scent behind the ears.

"We're going to do a polka," somebody called, "come dance with us. . . ."

"A bit of business first," Hencher said, and grinned over the heads at the woman. "A little business first—then we'll be the boys for you, never fear."

A broken bench with the name *Annie* carved into it, a bucket half-filled with sand, something made of brass and swinging, a discarded man's shirt snagged on the horn of a big cleat bolted to the deck and, overhead, high in a box on the wall of the pilot house, the running light flickering through the sea gloom. He felt the desertion, the wind, the coming of darkness as soon as he stepped from the saloon.

She's home now, she's thinking about her hubby now, she's asking the cat where's Michael off to, where's my Michael gone to?

He spat sharply over the rail, turned his jacket collar up, breathed on the dry bones of his hands.

Together, heads averted, going round the deck, coming abreast of the saloon and once more sheltered by a flapping canvas: Hencher lit a cigar while he himself stood grinning in through the lighted window at the crowd. He watched them kicking, twirling, holding hands, fitting their legs and feet to the steps of the dance; he grinned at the back of the girl too young to have a girdle to pull down, grinned at the boy in the black suit. He smelled the hot tobacco smell and Hencher was with him, Hencher who was fat and blowing smoke on the glass.

"You say you have a van, Hencher, a horse van. . . ."

"That's the ticket. Two streets over from this quay, parked in an alley by the ship-fitter's, as good a van as you'd want and with a full tank. And it's a van won't be recognized, I can tell you that. A little oil and sand over the name, you see. Like they did in the war. And we drive it wherever we please—you see—and no one's the wiser."

He nodded and for a moment, across the raven-blue and gold of the water, he saw the spires and smokestacks and tiny bridges of the city black as a row of needles burned and tipped with red. The tide had risen to its high mark and the gangway was nearly vertical; going down he burned his palm on the tarred rope, twice lost his footing. The engines were loud now. Except for Hencher and himself, except for the officer posted at the foot of the gangway and a seaman standing by each of the hawsers fore and aft, the quay was deserted, and when the sudden blasting of the ship's whistle commenced the timbers shook, the air was filled with steam, the noise of the whistle sounded through the quay's dark cargo shed. Then it stopped, except for the echoes in the shed and out on the water, and the man gave his head a shake as if he could not rid it of the whistling. He held up an unlighted cigarette and Hencher handed him the cigar.

"Oh," said the officer, "it's you two again. Find the lady in question all right?"

"We found her, Captain. She's comfy, thanks, good and comfy."

"Well, according to schedule we tie up here tomorrow morning at twenty past eight."

"My friend and me will come fetch her on the dot, Captain, good as my word. . . ."

Again the smothering whistle, again the sound of chain, and someone shouted through a megaphone and the gangway rose up on a cable; the seamen hoisted free the ropes, the bow of the *Artemis* began to swing, the officer stepped over the widening space between quay and ship and was gone.

"Come," said Hencher, and took hold of his arm, "we can watch from the shed."

They leaned against a crate under the low roof and there were rats and piles of dried shells and long dark empty spaces in the cargo shed. There were holes in the flooring: if he moved the toe of his shoe his foot would drop off into the water; if he moved his hand there would be the soft pinch of fur or the sudden burning of dirty teeth. Only Hencher and himself and the rats. Only scum, the greasy water and a punctured and sodden dory beneath them—filth for a man to fall into.

"There . . . she's got the current now. . . ."

He stared with Hencher toward the lights, small gallery of decks and silhouetted stacks that was the *Artemis* a quarter mile off on the river.

"They'll have their fun on that little ship tonight and with a moon, too, or I miss my guess. Another quarter hour," Hencher was twisting, trying for a look at his watch in the dark, "and I'll bring the lorry round."

Side by side, rigid against the packing crate, listening to the rats plop down, waiting, and all the while marking the disappearance of the excursion boat. Only the quay's single boom creaking in the wind and a view of the river across the now empty berth was left to them, while ahead of the *Artemis* lay a peaceful sea worn smooth by night and flotillas of landing boats forever beached. With beer and music in her saloon she was off there making for the short sea cliffs, for the moonlit coast and desolate windy promontories into which the batteries had once been built. At 3 A.M. her navigator discovering the cliffs, fixing location by sighting a flat tin helmet nailed to a stump on the tallest cliff's windy lip, and the *Artemis* would approach the shore, and all of them—boy, girl, lonely woman—would have a glimpse of ten miles of coast with an iron fleet half-sunk in the mud, a moonlit vision of windlasses, torpedo tubes, skein of rusted masts and the stripped hull of a destroyer rising stern first from that muddied coast under the cliffs. Beside the rail the lonely woman at least, and perhaps the rest of them, would see the ten white coastal miles, the wreckage safe from tides and storms and snowy nights, the destroyer's superstructure rising respectable as a lighthouse keeper's station. All won, all lost, all over, and for half a crown they could have it now, this seawreck and abandon and breeze of the ocean surrounding them. And the boy at least would hear the moist unjoyful voice of his girl while the *Artemis* remained off shore, would feel the claspknife in the pocket of her skirt and, down on the excursion boat's hard deck, would know the comfort to be taken with a young girl worn to thinness and wiry and tough as the titlings above the cliffs.

Michael stood rigid against the packing crate, alone. He waited deep within the shed and watched, sniffed something that was not of rats or cargo at all. Then he saw it drifting along the edges of the quay, rising up through the rat holes round his shoes: fog, the inevitable white hair strands which every night looped out across the river as if once each night the river must grow old, clammy, and in its age and during these late hours only, produce the thick miles of old woman's hair within whose heaps and strands it might then hide all bodies, tankers, or fat iron shapes nodding to themselves out there.

Fog of course and he should have expected it, should have carried a torch. Yet, whatever was to come his way would come, he knew, like this—slowly and out of a thick fog. Accidents, meetings unexpected, a figure emerging to put its arms about him: where to discover everything he dreamed of except in a fog. And, thinking of slippery corners, skin suddenly bruised, grappling hooks going blindly through the water: where to lose it all if not in the same white fog.

Alone he waited until the great wooden shed was filled with the fog that caused the rotting along the water's edge. His shirt was flat, wet against his chest. The forked iron boom on the quay was gone, and as for the two tankers that marked the vacated berth of the excursion boat, he knew they were there only by the dead sounds they made. All about him was the visible texture and density of the expanding fog. He was listening for the lorry's engine, with the back of a hand kept trying to wipe his cheek.

An engine was nearby suddenly, and despite the fog he knew that it was not Hencher's lorry but was the river barge approaching on the lifting tide. And he was alone, shivering, helpless to give a signal. He had no torch, no packet of matches. No one trusted a man's voice in a fog.

All the bells and whistles in mid-river were going at once, and hearing the tones change, the strokes change, listening to the metallic or compressed-air sounds of sloops or ocean-going vessels protesting their identities and their vague shifting locations on the whole of this treacherous and fog-bound river's surface—a horrible noise, a confused warning, a frightening celebration—he knew that only his own barge, of all this night's drifting or anchored traffic, would come without lights and making no sound except for the soft and faltering sound of the engine itself. This he heard—surely someone was tinkering with it, nursing it, trying to stop the loss of oil with a bare hand—and each moment he waited for even these illicit sounds to go dead. But in the fog the barge engine was turning over and, all at once, a man out there cleared his throat.

So he stood away from the packing crate and slowly went down to his hands and knees and discovered that he could see a little distance now, and began to crawl. He feared that the rats would get his hands; he ran his fingers round the crumbling edges of the holes; his creeping knee came down on fragments of a smashed bottle. There was an entire white sea-world floating and swirling in that enormous open door, and he crawled out to it.

"You couldn't do nothing about the bleeding fog!"

He had crossed the width of the quay, had got a grip on the iron joint of the boom and was trying to rise when the voice spoke up directly beneath him and he knew that if he fell it would not be into the greasy and squid-blackened water but onto the deck of the barge itself. He was unable to look down yet, but it was clear that the man who had spoken up at him had done so with a laugh, casually, without needing to cup his hands.

Before the man had time to say it again—"You couldn't do nothing about the bleeding fog, eh, Hencher? I wouldn't ordinarily step out of the house on a night like this"—the quay had already shaken beneath the van's tires and the headlamp had flicked on, suddenly, and hurt his eyes where he hung from the boom, one hand thrown out for balance and the other stuck like a dead man's to the iron. Hencher, carrying two bright lanterns by wire loops, had come between himself and the lorry's yellow headlamps—"Lively now, Mr. Banks," he was saying without a smile—and had thrust one of the lanterns upon him in time to reach out his freed hand and catch the end of wet moving rope on the instant it came lashing up from the barge. So that the barge was docked, held safely by the rope turned twice round a piling, when he himself was finally able to look straight down and see it, the long and blunt-nosed barge riding high in a smooth bowl scooped out of the fog. Someone had shut off the engine.

"Take a smoke now, Cowles—just a drag, mind you—and we'll get on with it."

She ought to see her hubby now. She ought to see me now.

He had got his arm through the fork of the boom and was holding the lantern properly, away from his body and down, and the glare from its reflector lighted the figure of the man Cowles below him and in cold wet rivulets drifted sternward down the length of the barge. Midships were three hatches, two battened permanently shut, the third covered by a sagging canvas. Beside this last hatch and on a bale of hay sat a boy naked from the waist up and wearing twill riding britches. In the stern was a small cabin. On its roof, short booted legs dangling over the edge, a jockey in full racing dress sat with a cigarette now between his lips and hands clasped round one of his tiny knees.

"Cowles! I want off . . . I want off this bloody coop!" he shouted.

The cigarette popped into his mouth then. It was a trick he had. The lips were pursed round the hidden cigarette and the little man was staring up not at Cowles or Hencher but at himself, and even while Cowles was ordering the two of them, boy and jockey, to get a hop on and drag the tarpaulin off the hold, the jockey kept looking up at him, toe of one little boot twitching left and right but the large bright eyes remaining fixed on his own—until the cigarette popped out again and the dwarfed man allowed himself to be helped from his seat on the cabin roof by the stableboy whose arms, in the lantern light, were upraised and spattered with oil to the elbows.

"Get a hop on now, we want no coppers or watchman or dock inspectors catching us at this bit of game. . . ."

The fog was breaking, drifting away, once more sinking into the river. Long shreds of it were wrapped like rotted sails or remnants of a wet wash round the buttresses and hand-railings of the bridges, and humped outpourings of fog came rolling from within the cargo shed as if all the fuels of this cold fire were at last consumed. The wind had started up again, and now the moon was low, just overhead.

"Here, use my bleeding knife, why don't you?"

The water was slimy with moonlight, the barge itself was slimy—all black and gold, dripping—and Cowles, having flung his own cigarette behind him and over the side, held the blade extended and moved down the slippery deck toward the boy and booted figure at the hatch with the slow embarrassed step of a man who at any moment expects to walk upon eel or starfish and trip, lose his footing, sprawl heavily on a deck as unknown to him as this.

"Here it is now, Mr. Banks!" He felt one of Hencher's putty hands quick and soft and excited on his arm. "Now you'll see what there is to see. . . ."

He looked down upon the naked back, the jockey's nodding cap, the big man Cowles and the knife stabbing at the ropes, until Cowles grunted and the three of them pulled off the tarpaulin and he was staring down at all the barge carried in its hold: the black space, the echo of bilge and, without movement, snort, or pawing of hoof, the single white marble shape of the horse, whose neck (from where he leaned over, trembling, on the quay) was the fluted and tapering neck of some serpent, while the head was an elongated white skull with nostrils, eye sockets, uplifted gracefully in the barge's hold —*Draftsman by Emperor's Hand out of Shallow Draft by Amulet, Castle Churl by Draftsman out of Likely Castle by Cold Masonry, Rock Castle by Castle Churl out of Words on Rock by Plebeian . . . until tonight when he's ours, until tonight when he's ours. . . .*

"Didn't I tell you, Mr. Banks? Didn't I? Good as his word, that's Hencher."

The whistles died one by one on the river and it was not Wednesday at all, only a time slipped off its cycle with hours and darkness never to be accounted for. There was water viscous and warm that lapped the sides of the barge; a faint up and down motion of the barge which he could gauge against the purple rings of a piling; and below him the still crouched figures of the men and, in its moist alien pit, the silver horse with its ancient head, round which there buzzed a single fly as large as his own thumb and molded of shining blue wax.

He stared down at the lantern-lit blue fly and at the animal whose two ears were delicate and unfeeling, as unlikely to twitch as two pointed fern leaves etched on glass, and whose silver coat gleamed with the colorless fluid of some ghostly libation and whose decorous drained head smelled of a violence that was his own.

Even when he dropped the lantern—"No harm done, no harm done," Hencher said quickly—the horse did not shy or throw itself against the ribs of the barge, but remained immobile, fixed in the same standing posture of rigorous sleep that they had found it in at the moment the tarpaulin was first torn away. Though Cowles made his awkward lunge to the rail, saw what it was—lantern with cracked glass half sunk, still burning on the water, then abruptly turning dark and sinking from sight—and laughed through his nose, looked up at them: "Bleeding lot of help he is. . . ."

"No harm done," said Hencher again, sweating and by light of the van's dim headlamps swinging out the arm of the boom until the cable and hook were correctly positioned above the barge's hold. "Just catch the hook, Cowles, guide it down."

Without a word, hand that had gripped the lantern still trembling, he took his place with Hencher at the iron bar which, given the weight of Hencher and himself, would barely operate the cable drum. He got his fingers round the bar; he tried to think of himself straining at such a bar, but it was worse for Hencher, whose heart was sunk in fat. Yet Hencher too was ready—in tight shirtsleeves, his jacket removed and hanging from the tiny silver figure of a winged man that adorned the van's radiator cap—so that he himself determined not to let go of the bar as he had dropped the lantern but, instead, to carry his share of the horse's weight, to stay at the bar and drum until the horse could suffer this last transport. There was no talking on the barge. Only sounds of their working, plash of the boy's feet in the bilge, the tinkle of buckles and strap ends as the webbed bands were slid round the animal's belly and secured.

Hencher was whispering: "Ever see them lift the bombs out of the craters? Two or three lads with a tripod, some lengths of chain, a few red flags and a rope to keep the children away . . . then cranking up the unexploded bomb that would have bits of debris and dirt sticking peacefully as you please to that filthy big cylinder . . . something to see, men at a job like that and fishing up a live bomb big enough to blow a cathedral to the ground." Then, feeling a quiver: "But here now, lay into it gently, Mr. Banks, that's the ticket."

He pushed—Hencher was pushing also—until after a moment the drum stopped and the cable that stretched from the tip of the boom's arm down to the ring swiveling above the animal's webbed harness was taut.

"O.K." It was Cowles kneeling at the hold's edge, speaking softly and clearly on the late night air, "O.K. now . . . up he goes."

The barge, which could support ten tons of coal or gravel on the river's oily and slop-sullied tide, was hardly lightened when the horse's hoofs swung a few inches free of that planking hidden and awash. But drum, boom, cable and arms could lift not a pound more than this, and lifted this—the weight of the horse—only with strain and heat, pressure and rusted rigidity. Though his eyes were closed he knew when the boom swayed, could feel the horse beginning to sway off plumb. He heard the drum rasping round, heard the loops of rusted cable wrapping about the hot drum one after another, slowly.

"Steady now, steady . . . he's bloody well high enough."

Then, as Hencher with burned hands grasped the wheel that would turn the boom its quarter circle and position the horse over quay, not over barge, he felt a fresh wind on his cheek and tilted his head, opened his eyes, and saw his second vision of the horse: up near the very tip of the iron arm, rigid and captive in the sling of two webbed bands, legs stiff beneath it, tail blown out straight on the wind and head lifted—they had wrapped a towel round the eyes—so that high in the air it became the moonlit spectacle of some giant weather vane. And seeing one of the front legs begin to move, to lift, and the hoof—that destructive hoof—rising up and dipping beneath the slick shoulder, seeing this slow gesture of the horse preparing to paw suddenly at the empty air, and feeling the tremor through his fingers still lightly on the bar: "Let him down, Hencher, let him down!" he cried, and waved both hands at the blinded and hanging horse even as it began to descend.

Until the boom regained its spring and balance like a tree spared from a gale; until the drum, released, clattered and in its rusty mechanism grew still; until the four sharp hoofs touched wood of the quay. Cowles—first up the ladder and followed by Jimmy Needles the jockey and Lovely the stableboy—reached high and loosed the fluttering towel from round its eyes. The boy approached and snapped a lead-rope to the halter and the jockey, never glancing at the others or at the horse, stepped up behind him, whispering: "Got a fag for Needles, mister? Got a fag for Needles?" Not until this moment when he shouted, "Hencher, don't leave me, Hencher . . ." and saw the fat naked arm draw back and the second lantern sail in an arc over the water, and in a distance also saw the white hindquarters on the van's ramp and dark shapes running—not until this moment was he grateful for the little hard cleft of fingers round his arm and the touch of the bow-legged figure still begging for his fag but pulling and guiding him at last in the direction of the cab's half-open door. Cowles had turned the petcocks and behind them the barge was sinking.

These five rode crowded together on the broad seat, five white faces behind a rattling windscreen. Five men with elbows gnawing at elbows, hands and pairs of boots confused, men breathing hard and remaining silent except for Hencher who complained he hadn't room to drive. In labored first gear and with headlights off, they in the black van traveled the slow bumping distance down the length of the cargo shed, from plank to rotted plank moved slowly in the van burdened with their own weight and the weight of the horse until at the corner of the deserted building—straight ahead lay darkness that was water and all five, smelling sweat and river fumes and petrol, leaned forward together against the dim glass—they turned and drove through an old gate topped with a strand of barbed wire and felt at last hard rounded cobblestones beneath the tires.

"No one's the wiser now, lads," said Hencher, and laughed, shook the sweat from his eyes, took a hand off the wheel and slapped Cowles' knee. "We're just on a job if anyone wants to know," smiling, both fat hands once more white on the wheel. "So we've only to sit tight until we make Highland Green . . . eh, Cowles . . . eh, Needles . . . eh, Mr. Banks?"

But Michael himself, beneath the jockey and pressed between Cowles' thick flank and the unupholstered door, was tasting lime: smells of the men, smells of oil, lingering smells of the river and now, faint yet definite, seeping through the panel at his back, smells of the horse—all these mixed odors filled his mouth, his stomach, and some hard edge of heel or brake lever or metal that thrust down from the dash was cutting into his ankle, hurting the bone. Under his buttocks he felt the crooked shape of a spanner; from a shelf behind the thin cushions straw kept falling; already the motor was overheated and they were driving too fast in the darkness of empty shopping districts and areas of cheap lodgings with doorways and windows black except for one window, seven or eight streets ahead of them, in which a single light would be burning. And each time this unidentified black shabby van went round a corner he felt the horse—his horse—thump against one metal side or the other. Each time the faint sound and feel of the thumping made him sick.

"Hencher. I think you had better leave me off at the flat."

Then trying to breathe, trying to explain, trying to argue with Hencher in the speeding overheated cab and twisting, seeing the fluted dark nostril at a little hole behind the driver's head. Until Hencher smiled his broad worried smile and in a loud voice said: "Oh well, Mr. Banks is a married man," speaking to Cowles, the jockey, the stableboy, nudging Cowles in the ribs. "And you must always make allowance for a married man. . . ."

Cowles yawned, and, as best he could, rubbed his great coatsleeves still wet from the spray. "Leave him off, Hencher, if he gives us a gander at the wife."

The flat door is open and the cat sleeps. Just inside the door, posted on a straight chair, market bag at her feet and the cat at her feet, sitting with the coat wrapped round her shoulders and the felt hat still on her head: there she waits, waits up for him. The neighbor on the chair next to her is sleeping—like the cat—and the mouth is half-open with the breath hissing through, and the eyes are buried under curls. But her own eyes are level, the lids red, the face smooth and white and soft as soap. Waiting up for him.

Without moving, without taking her eyes from the door: "Where's Michael off to? Where's my Michael gone?" she asks the cat. Then down the outer hall, in the dark of the one lamp burning, she hears the click of the house key, the sound of the loose floor board, and she thinks to raise a hand and dry her cheek. With the same hand she touches her neighbor's arm.

"It's all right, Mrs. Stickley," she whispers, "he's home now."

The engine is boiling over when the van reaches Highland Green. Water flows down the dented black hood, the grille, and a jet of steam bursting up from the radiator scalds the wings of the tiny silver figure of the man which, in attitude of pursuit, flies from the silver cap. Directly before the machine and in the light of the headlamps Hencher stands shielding his face from the steam. Then moves quickly, throws his belly against the hot grille, catches the winged figure in a rag and gives it a twist.

"Come along, cock, we haven't got all the bleeding night," says Cowles.

It is dark in Highland Green, dark in this public stable which lies so close to the tanks and towers of the gasworks that a man, if he wished, might call out to the old watchman there. Dark at 3 A.M. and quiet; no one tends the stables at night and only a few spiritless horses for hire are drowsing in a few of the endless stalls. Hardly used now, dead at night, with stray dogs and little starved birds making use of the stalls, and weeds choking the yard. Refuse fills the well, there is a dry petrol pump near a loft building intended for hay.

Hencher steps out of the headlamp's beam, drops the radiator cap, throws the rag to the ground, soothes his hand with his lips. "You needn't tell me to hurry, Cowles," he says, and kicks the tiny winged man away from him into the dead potash and weeds.

Hencher hears the whistles then—two long, a short—and all at once straightens his cap, gives a last word to Cowles: "Leave the animal in the van until I return. And no noise now, mind you. . . ." From beneath the musty seat in the cab he takes a long torch and walks quickly across the rutted yard. Behind him the jockey is puffing on a fresh cigarette, the stableboy—thinking of a girl he once saw bare to the flesh—is resting his head against a side of the van, and Cowles in the dark is frowning and moving his stubby fingers across the watch chain that is a dull gold weight on his vest.

Once in the loft building Hencher lights the torch. Presses the switch with his thumb but keeps the torch down, is careful not to shine the beam toward the exact spot where he knows the man is standing. Rather lights himself with the torch and walks ahead into the dark. He is smiling though he feels sweat on his cheeks and in the folds of his neck. The loft building smells of creosote, the dead pollen of straw, and petrol. He cannot see it, but he knows that to his left there is a double door, closed, and beside it, hidden and waiting within the darkness, a passenger car stately with black lacquer and a radiator cap identical to that on the van. If he swings the torch, flashes it suddenly and recklessly to the left, he knows the light will be dashed back in his face from the car's thick squares of polished window glass. But he keeps the beam at his heel, walks more and more slowly until at last he stops.

"You managed to get here, Hencher," the man says.

"I thought I was on the dot, Larry . . . good as my word, you know."

"Yes, always good as your word. But you've forgotten to take off your cap."

Hencher takes it off, feels his whole head exposed and hot and ugly. At last he allows himself to look, and it is only the softest glow that his torch sheds on the man before him.

"We got the horse, right outside in the van . . . I told you, right outside."

"But you stopped. You did not come here directly."

"I did my best. I did my bloody best, but if he wants to knock it off, if he wants to stop at home and have a word with the wife, why that's just unfortunate . . . but no fault of mine, is it, Larry?"

And then, listening in the direction of the car, waiting for a sound—scratch of the ignition key, oiled suck of gear-lever—he sees the hand extended in front of him and is forced to take hold of it. One boot moves, the other moves, the trenchcoat makes a harsh rubbing noise. And the hand lets go of his, the man fades out of the light and yet—Hencher wipes his face and listens—once in the darkness the footsteps ring back to him like those of an officer on parade.

He keeps his own feet quiet until he reaches the yard and sees the open night sky beginning to change and grow milky like chemicals in a vat, and until he sniffs a faint odor of dung and tobacco smoke. Then he trudges loudly as he can and suddenly, calling the name, shines the bright torch on Cowles.

"Pissed off, was he," says Cowles, and does not blink.

But in the cab Hencher already braces the steering wheel against his belly; the driver's open door swings to the movement of the van. Cowles and the jockey and stableboy walk in slow procession behind the van, which is not too wide for the overgrown passage between the row of stalls, the long dark space between the low stable buildings, but which is high so that now and again the roof of the van brushes then scrapes against the rotted eaves. The tires are wet from the dampness of tangled and prickly weeds. Once, the van stops and Hencher climbs down, drags a bale of molded hay from its path. Then they move—horse van, walking men—and exhaust fumes fill empty bins, water troughs, empty stalls. In darkness they pass a shovel in an iron wheelbarrow, a saddle pad covered with inert black flies, a whip leaning against a whited post. Round a corner they come upon a red lantern burning beside an open and freshly whitewashed box stall. The hay rack has been mended, clean hard silken straw covers the floor, a red horse blanket lies folded on a weathered cane chair near the lantern.

"Lovely will fetch him down for you, Hencher," says Cowles.

"I will fetch him down myself, if you please."

And Lovely the stableboy grins and walks into the stall; the jockey pushes the horse blanket off the chair, sits down heavily; Cowles takes one end of the chain while Hencher works with the other.

They pry up the ends of the chain, allow it to fall link upon ringing link into bright iron pools at their feet until the raised and padded ramp swings loose, opens wider and wider from the top of the van as Cowles and Hencher lower it slowly down. Two gray men who stand with hands on hips and look up into the interior of the van. It is dark in there, steam of the horse drifts out; it appears that between the impacted bright silver flesh of the horse and padded walls no space exists for a man.

Hencher puts the unlighted cigar between his teeth and steps onto the ramp. Silent and nearly broad as the horse he climbs up the ramp, gets his footing, squeezes himself against the white and silver flesh—the toe of one boot striking a hoof on edge, both hands attempting to hold off the weight of the horse—then glances down at Cowles, tries to speak, and slides suddenly into the dark of the van.

And Cowles shouts, doubles over then as powerless as Hencher in the van. The ramp bounces, shakes on its hinges, and though the brake holds and the wheels remain locked, the chassis, cab, and high black sides all sway forward once at the moment they absorb that first unnatural motion of horse lunging at trapped man. Shakes, rattles, and the first loud sound of the hoof striking its short solid blow to metal fades. But not the commotion, the blind forward swaying of the van. While Cowles is shouting for help and dodging, leaping away, he somehow keeps his eyes on the visible rear hoofs and sees that, long as it lasts—the noise, the directionless pitching of the van—those rear hoofs never cease their dancing. The horse strikes a moment longer, but there is no metallic ringing, no sharp sound, and only the ramp drags a little more and the long torch falls from the cab.

Then Cowles is vomiting into the tall grass—he is a fat man and a man as fat as himself lies inside the van —and the grass is sour, the longest blades tickle his lips. On his knees he sweats, continues to be sick, and with large distracted hands keeps trying to fold the grass down upon the whiteness collecting in the hollow of bare roots.

Hencher, with fat lifeless arms still raised to the head kicked in, huddles yet on the van's narrow floor, though the horse is turning round and round in the whitewashed stall. The jockey has left his chair and, cigarette between his lips, dwarfed legs apart, stands holding the long torch in both his hands and aiming it—like a rifle aimed from the hip—at Cowles. While Lovely the stableboy is singing now in a young pure Irish voice to the horse.

"Give me a hand with the body, Cowles, and we'll drag it into the stall," the jockey says. "Can't move it alone, cock, can't move it alone."

2

SIDNEY SLYTER SAYS

Fastest Track at Aldington Since War . . .

Thirteen Horses to Take the Field . . .

Rock Castle Remains Question in Reporter's Mind . . .

Oh Mrs. Laval, Oh Sybilline . . . Your Mr. Slyter has all the luck you'll say! Well, we drank each other's health again last night, and she confessed that she knew me right along, and I told her that everyone knows Mr. Sidney Slyter, your old professional. I never lose sight of love or money in my prognostications, do I now? But it's business first for me. . . . A puzzling late entry is Rock Castle, owned by one Mr. Michael Banks. And here's the dodge: if the entry is actually Rock Castle as the owner claims, then I know him to be a horse belonging to the stables of that old sporting dowager, Lady Harvey-Harrow, and how does he come to be entered under the colors (lime-green and black) of Mr. Banks? Something suspicious here, something for the authorities or I miss my guess. However, I shall speak with Mr. Banks; I shall look at the horse; I shall telephone the dowager. Meanwhile, Sidney Slyter says: wish you were here. . . .

It was Tuesday next and Margaret began to miss Michael in the afternoon. She tried to nap, but the pillow kept slipping through her fingers; she tried to mend the curtain, but her knees were in the way of the needle. Something was coming toward the window and it made her lonely. She went to the closet and from behind the duster and pail took down Banks' bottle of spirits and drank a very small glass of it. The missing of Michael came over her, the loneliness, the small grief, and she was drifting quickly down the day and time itself was wandering.

"Here puss, here puss. . . ."

Limping, bristling its hairs, the cat appeared near the pantry door. It ate quickly, choked on every mouthful, the head jerked up and down. The silver of the fish and speckles of the cat's eye caught the light. Now and then the dish scraped a little on the floor. Her back to the window, kneeling, Margaret watched the animal eat. And the cat, creature that claws tweed, sits high in the hallway, remains incorrigible upon the death of its mistress, beds itself in the linen or thrusts its enormous head into an alley, now sucked and gagged on the fish as if drawing a peculiar sweetness from the end of a thin bone.

But there was nothing sweet for her. She had dropped crumbs for the birds, she had leaned from the window, she had given the cat its dish. In the window—it looked out on the laundry court, was hard to raise—she had smelled the cool drifting air of spring and glanced at wireless antennas pulled taut across the sky. Annie must have heard the frame crash up, or must have caught the sound of her humming. Because Annie had come to the adjoining window, thrust out her blonde head, at twenty past two had jammed her sharp red elbows on the sill and talked for a while.

"Rotten day," Annie had said to her.

"Michael mentioned it would be clear."

"It's a rotten day. How's his horse?"

"Oh, he's a fine horse. A lovely horse. . . ."

"I don't know who Mike thinks he is, to go off and get himself a horse. But I've always wanted to kiss a jockey."

And Annie had taken up a little purse and counted her change in the window. Together they had heard a tram eating away its tracks, heard the hammer and hawking of the world on the other side of the building. It was spring in the sunlight and they leaned toward each other, and the smell of cooking mutton had come into the courtyard.

Now, between three and six, there was nothing sweet for her. Even her friend Annie had left the flat next door, and Michael was gone.

"I'm dead to the world," she said aloud.

Behind cataracts of pale eyes the cat looked across at her, cat with a black and yellow head which a good milliner, in years past, might have sewn to the front of a woman's high-crowned feathered hat. Margaret scratched on the floor, for a moment smiled. Her cat circled round the dish. It was so dark now that she could not see into the kitchen. From somewhere a draft began blowing the bottom of her skirt and she wondered what a fortuneteller—one of those old ladies with red hair and a birthmark—would make of her at this moment. There was the beef broth, water to be drawn and boiled, the sinister lamp to light, a torn photograph of children by the sea. Cold laurels in this empty room.

"He has only gone to look at the horse in Highland Green," she said. "It isn't far."

Once the madame of a frock shop had tried to dress her in pink. And even she, Margaret, had at the last minute before the gown was packed, denied the outrageous combination of herself and the color. Once an Italian barber had tried to kiss her and she had escaped the kiss. Once Michael had given her an orchid preserved in a glass ball, and now she could not find it. How horrible she felt in pink; how horrible the touch of the barber's lips; how heavy was the glassed orchid on her breast.

Feeling lucky? Soon Michael would ask her that, after the sink was empty and her apron off. It was never luck she felt but she would smile.

In the darkness the cat swallowed the last flake of herring—Michael usually fed it, Michael understood how it wanted an old woman's milk to drink—then disappeared. It was gone and she thought it had left her in search of the whispering tongue of some old woman in a country cottage. So she stood, picked up the dish, made her way toward the smells of yellow soap and blackened stove. There was a bulb in the kitchen. But the bulb was bleak, it spoiled the brown wood, the sink, the cupboard doors which she had covered with blue curtains. She washed the cat's dish in the dark, lit the stove in the dark. For a moment, before the match flame caught at the sooted jets, she smelled the cold endless odor of greasy gas and her heart commenced suddenly to beat.

"Michael. Michael, is it you?"

But she turned, struck a second match, and the gas flames puffed up from the pipe in a circle like tiny blue teeth round the rim of a coronet and she herself was plain, only a girl who could cook, clean, sing a little. And then, in the light of the gas, she saw a stableboy's thin face and, outside, the mortuary bells were ringing.

. . . The thin face of a pike and dirty hands—not black by earth, soot, or grease, but the soiled tan color of hands perpetually rubbing down a horse's skin—and wearing riding trousers of twill but no socks, and from the belt up, naked.

"Now then, Mr. Hencher's with the horse, is that it?"

Together they walk in the direction of the stalls, passing a shovel in an iron wheelbarrow, a saddle pad covered with black flies, a whip leaning against a whited post. Over one stall, on a rusty nail, hangs a jockey's faded green-and-yellow cap.

They continue and from the rotted wood in the eaves overhead comes the sound, compact, malcontent, of a hive of bees stinging to death a sparrow. And the stableboy, treading hay wisps and manure between his shoes and the stones, points to the closed stalls and tells him of Princess Pat, Islam, Dead-at-Night, the few mares and stallions within. And he hears them paw the dark, hears the slow scraping of four pointed hoofs.

"Smoke, Mr. Banks? I'll just have a drag or two before I go back in with him."

A growth of wild prickly briar climbs one side of the stall. There are no sounds within. Michael steps away, draws in his cuff, stares at the double doors—while the stableboy shoots back the bolt, slips inside. The horse stands head to the rear wall, and first he sees the streaks of the animal's buttocks, the high point that descends to the back. Then he sees the polished outline of the legs. Then the tail.

And at the same moment, under the tail's heavy and graying gall, and between the hind legs, he sees Hencher's outstretched body and, nearest himself, the inert shoes, toes down.

"How do you like him, Mr. Banks? Fine horse, eh?"

"Hencher," he whispers, "here's Hencher!"

Together they will bury Hencher with handfuls of straw, bolt the doors, wipe their hands, and for himself there will be no cod or beef at six, no kissing her at six, no going home—not with Hencher kicked to death by the horse. And forward in the dark the neck is lowered and he sees the head briefly as it swings sideways at the level of the front hoofs with ears drawn back and great honey-colored eyes floating out to him.

She heard the distant mortuary bells. Outside, over all this part of the city, returning fathers were using their weary keys. It was time to feed the cats, the dogs, the little broken dolls. It was never luck she felt, but Margaret waited, standing beside the coal grate in which they built no fire, waited for him to hang up his hat, untie her apron strings. When Banks had first kissed her, touching the arm that was only an arm, the cheek that was only a cheek, he had turned away to find a hair in his mouth.

Feeling lucky?

In how many minutes now she would nod, smile again, sit across from him and hold her pencil and the evening five-pound crostic, she wearing no rings except the wedding band and, in her otherwise straight brown hair, touching the single deep wave which she had saved from childhood.

Now and again from out the window would come the sound of lorries, the beat of the solitary policeman's step, the cry of a child. Later, after he had pulled the light string, she would dream of the crostics and, in the dark, men with numbers wrapped round their fingers would feel her legs, or she would lie with an obscure member of the government on a leather couch, trying to remember and all the while begging for his name. Later still the cat would come licking about for its old woman's milk.

The asparagus was boiling finally when the telephone rang. She groped, found the instrument in the hallway, did not let the receiver touch her ear. "Yes?" And even after the first words were spoken the bell continued to ring, a mad thing ringing and ringing, trying to rouse the darkened flat.

". . . the telephone's broken," she whispered into the cup, and her hand was shaking. Then it went out of her head suddenly, and there was only the dark terrible dustiness in the hall.

"Margaret?"

"Michael, is it you?"

"It is. Have you turned down the stove?"

"I think so, Michael."

"And the water off?"

"I think so."

"Good."

"Are you all right, Michael?"

"We're going up," and the voice was fainter now. "We're going up for the Aldington. There's a hundred thousand in it. . . ."

"I want to come," she said.

There was a pause. And then: "I've thought of that. There's always the train. You come by train. Tonight."

"Annie might join me if I asked her."

"Come alone. Just come alone."

"Yes, Michael."

After another pause: "You're the dear," he said softly in the dark with traces of tenderness, and she heard the click and a child wailing somewhere down the row.

"You're the dear," she repeated to herself in the kitchen. But she had not turned off the stove and the asparagus was burned. She put a little water in the pot and left it. An hour later she locked the flat, went down the stoop, signaled a high-topped taxicab to carry her to the train at Dreary Station. Hurrying she gave no thought to people on the streets. She was a girl with a band on her finger and poor handwriting, and there was no other world for her. No bitters in a bar, slick hair, smokes, no checkered vests. She was Banks' wife by the law, she was Margaret, and if the men ever did get hold of her and go at her with their truncheons or knives or knuckles, she would still be merely Margaret with a dress and a brown shoe, still be only a girl of twenty-five with a deep wave in her hair.

A wife would always ride through the night if she were bidden. Would ride through rainstorm, villages like Wimble, through woodland all night long. All of it for Michael's sake: the station, the sign at the end of the village, the cart with the single suitcase on it, the lantern swinging beyond the unfamiliar spout, the great shadows of this countryside. It was a lonely transport, there was a loose pin under her clothes. And in this world of carriage seats, vibrations, windows rattling, she stared at the other passenger, at the woman who had called something out to her in Dreary Station and followed her aboard the train.

A sudden roll of smoke passed the windows and she saw herself, and her eyes ached and already she had been in her clothes too long. But the crostics would be waiting when she returned. "What have you done with the kiddies, Mrs. Banks?" asked the woman again.

Beyond the lights of crossings it was dark, the trees bent away from the train, and Margaret felt the wobbling tracks running over the ties, and each tie crushed under the wheels became a child. Children were tied down the length of track: she saw the toads hopping off their bodies at the first whisper of wheels, the faint rattling of oncoming rods and chains, and she saw the sparks hitting the pale heads and feet. Then the steam lay behind on the tracks and the toads returned.

"Done with them?" Margaret said. "I've done nothing with them. There aren't any children."

The handle was rattling on her valise—she had not put it in the rack—and her toes pressed against a sooty pipe. Her brown skirt was drawn down completely, cloth over anonymous knees and heavy calves. In her hand was the pink ticket. She sat backward with her shoulder blades to the whistle engine, and looking out the window, she feared this reversed and disappearing countryside.

"Oh," said the woman and flattened her paper, "I thought you'd probably parked them with your mother."

"No. I didn't do anything like that."

"Weren't you ever parked when you were a child?"

"I don't remember. . . ."

"I was. I remember it," said the woman. "I was parked out more than I was home. For me there was nothing at the window, I used to eat my hands in the corner."

"I don't remember much of when I was a child," said Margaret. She noticed then a dead wasp suspended between the window's double sheets of glass. The train turned sharply and the overnight bag fell against her leg.

"Well," the woman spoke up above the noise. "Well," and coldly she reached a hand toward Margaret, "it used to be parking out for me." The woman paused, steadied herself, the train hissed round the turn. "But that's past. Now it's my sister leaves her kids with me of a weekend or summer. And I'm at the good end, now."

"All summer long?" asked Margaret.

"Some years, she does. I encourage it." And Margaret saw the wheels flattening the heads and feet.

A signal flashed. A yellow light then red, and levers, long prongs, pig-iron fingers worked in rust out there. The train swayed and stale water splashed in the decanters. The train smelled like the inside of an old man's hat—smelled of darkness, hair, tobacco—and the steam was up and she saw a car with its tiny lamps like match heads off in the blackness at a crossing. Were they merely waiting in the car? Or had the hand brake been set and were they kissing? Margaret felt the soot sifting into her bosom, she was breathing it down her nostrils. She wanted a wash.

"How old are they? Your sister's, I mean . . . her little children."

"Oh, young," said the woman, and Margaret looked at her. "But not so young they won't remember when they've grown. . . ." There were smells coming off the woman too, smells that lived on her despite the odor of coke and burning rails. Smells of shoe black and rotting lace, smells that were never killed by cleaning nor destroyed by the rain. The woman's strong body, her clothing, her hatpins and hair—all were greased with the smells of age.

"Monica's in the middle. Seven. She paints her nails."

"It's a nice name," said Margaret, and looking up,

saw the woman's eyes like a female warden's eyes, black, almost beside each other, set into tiny spectacles with tweezers.

There were coffins in the baggage car and all through the night she smelled the cushions with their faint odor of skin tonic and old people's basketry and felt the woman watching her—wide-awake—and it was dark and stifling, a journey that made her muscles sore. The light began to swing on its cord.

The train had stopped. The door handle went down suddenly—after how long, she thought. Then the door opened and she saw the figure of a man who was standing on some country station ramp with the steam round his legs and a wet face. Margaret saw the night behind the man, heard the far-off ring of spanners or hammer heads against the locomotive's high black dripping wheels at the front of the train. The man was big, heavy as a horse cart of stone; there was not a wrinkle in his trenchcoat over the shoulders, his chest was that of a boxer. He blocked the door, held it, and his head came through. Hatless, dark hair, large straight nose. In one hand was a cigarette and he flicked the ash quickly into the skirts of his coat, as if he had no business smoking on the job. He swayed, leaned, his neck was red. He looked at the woman, and then at her; there was a movement in the dark eyes.

"All right now, Little Dora?" Nerve ends crossed in his gray cheek, it was a low conservative voice for kindness or bad weather.

"Right enough," said the woman without moving her hands. Her chin was squared. Then: "But I could do with a smoke," she added, and turned her spectacles toward Margaret.

"You don't mind if Little Dora takes one, do you, Miss?" He looked at Margaret, spoke to her from the empty ramp. His tie was loose and he was an impassive escort who, by chance, could touch a woman's breast in public easily, with propriety, offending no one. "You don't mind, Miss?" And there was nothing hushed in the voice, no laughter in the eyes, only the man's voice itself and his rainswept cheek and the cliff of his head with the old razor nicks, to startle her.

"It's all right, Larry, don't push it. I can wait," said the woman. "Seen this item, have you?" She tapped her newspaper, watched him. A short cough of the whistle swept back over them like smoke.

He leaned forward, holding the door, gripping the jamb, and the shoes were blackened, everything neat about the socks, the gray gloves were softly buttoned about the wrists and the hair was smooth. Only the hint of the tie was disreputable; it was red silk and loosened round the neck.

"I don't mind smoking," said Margaret quietly.

She followed them, and the man put up his collar against the wind and coldness of the night's storm. Down the wet planking, down the train's whole length of iron, walking and through her tears now looking at the heads asleep behind the train's dim and dripping windows. The rain had stopped, but there was a good wind. Despite it she thought she heard laughter and, farther on, the sounds of an infant crying and sucking too. In a brace on the wall of the station master's hut was a rusty ax; directly over the top of the engine she saw a few stars. But she was cold, so dreadfully cold.

"Bloody wild," the man said softly into her ear.

He was on one side of her, the woman on the other. The man took hold of her arm as if to escort her firmly, safely, through a crowd of men; the woman caught her by the hand. She breathed, was filled with the smell of the fog, saw the woman dart her cigarette into the night. At the platform's sudden edge, she saw a field sunk like iron under the stone fences, a shape that might have been a murdered horse or sheep, a brook run cold. The soot was acrid, it drove against her cheeks; the smell of oil was heavy in its packing and under it lay the faint odor of manure and wet hay and gorse.

"Feeling better?"

But she could not answer him. The wind had not disturbed his collar, he never blinked, eyelids insensitive to the rush of air.

"Larry," the woman plucked at his sleeve, shouted, "What have you on for tomorrow?" She clutched her spectacles, the lace was torn at her throat.

"Not much," putting his arm down upon her, round her, "sleep late . . . get Sparrow to do my boots . . . drive out to the Damps, perhaps. . . ."

"And come by the Roost?" she shouted.

"I'll look in on you, Dora. . . ."

Then his loose red tie was caught by the wind. It came

out of the coat suddenly, and the red tip beat over the mist and thistles and wind off the end of the ramp. He waited a moment and carefully shut it away again.

"Had enough?" he asked.

They took her back down to the glass-and-iron door left open in the night, and she saw that it was the correct number on the door. With his hand still on her arm, and looking in as he had at first: "I expect you'll be wanting to see Mr. Banks tomorrow, Miss? Look sharp for him, Miss. That's my advice," and the woman laughed. When he stepped away, cupped his cigarette from view, once more the train began to move and the man stood waiting for his own door to be pulled abreast of him.

It was a good crowd. Margaret and the woman climbed down together. Men pushed close to the standing train and reached up, while steam boiled round their trouser legs, to tap the windows with their canes. The coffins went by on their separate trucks. Women with their stockings crooked, men with their coats wrinkled—sounds of leather, wood, laughter, and a bell still tolling. There were beef posters, hack drivers displaying their licenses, a fellow drinking from a brown pint bottle. Suddenly she felt the woman taking hold of her hand.

"Where will Michael be?" asked Margaret then, surrounded by the searching crowd. A stray dog passed after the coffins. For a moment she saw the man in the trenchcoat and his broad belt. He made a sign to the woman and, with three others dressed like himself, went under an arch to hire a car. On a wall was pasted an unillustrated poster: *You Can Win If You Want To.*

"Little Dora," a young woman was calling to them, "Dora!" She had red hair, dark near the crown. Her restless fingers touched the shoulder of a child whose hair was fastened with an elastic.

"You here too?"

"For the weekend only," the little girl's mother said, and fluffed her hair up on one side, kissed the woman's cheek. "But fancy you . . . such luck!"

"What's footing it, Sybilline?"

"It's the sunshine I want only," she said, holding the small girl's collar, "a rum, a toss, a look through a fellow's binoculars. . . . Will you take her, Dora?"

And after the child had changed hands: "This is Monica," she said to Margaret.

Margaret lost the far-off smell of grass when they went up the stairs. She had smelled it, wondered about it, sniffed it, the fresh clipped odor, the living exhalation of earth green and vast, a springtime of wet and color beyond the town's steam baths and shops and gaming rooms and the petrol pumps wedged between shuttered houses and hotels. Out there, over the steeple, over the wires, the wash, was the great green of the racecourse: the Damps. The grass itself; several ponds; the enormous stands with flags; the oval of roses in which men were murdered and where there fluttered torn-up stubs and a handkerchief—Margaret had tasted the green and then it was gone. Now the door closed and she smelled cheap marmalade and the rubber of pharmaceutical apparatus for home use. A small trunk stood by the door to the room. The woman, Dora, had a key in her hand.

"You seem to know the place, Little Dora."

"It's the first time for me."

"How then . . ."

"It's like all the rest."

The room was on the second floor. White, large, it had a closet with a sink in it. There were two brass beds covered with sheets, a picture of a girl in a lake. It was clean, but a pair of braces had been forgotten near the window.

3

SIDNEY SLYTER SAYS

Candy Stripe Looks Good . . .

Marlowe's Pippet Still Picked to Win . . .

Owner Refuses Comment on Rock Castle . . .

. . . extremely popular several seasons back. Well, Slyter excused himself from Mrs. Laval last night and talked by telephone to Lady Harvey-Harrow's groom. I couldn't reach the Manor House hence requested the stables, and Crawley the groom—he's as old as the dowager herself—Crawley said he had no recollection of the horse. That was his phrase exactly. (Heard stable rats nibbling corn in the background while Crawley tried to make it clear that his Lady, who might remember something helpful, had fallen off to sleep in the Manor House at sundown and could not be called.) Your Sidney Slyter will not take no. . . . Must drive to the estate. . . . Mrs. Laval just laughed—Oh Sybilline's lovely laugh—and said I should forget about Rock Castle. But what do women know of such mysteries? Slyter's got his public to consider. . . . This afternoon I confronted the enigmatic Mr. Banks coming out of the Men's and offered him my

> hand, saying Slyter's the name. But he was white as my carnation and trembling; said he had no words for the Press; claimed he had an engagement with a lady, and I laughed at that. No apologies. I told him my readers were betting on Marlowe's Pippet to win, and let him pass. . . . I want to know what's the matter with Mr. Banks. I want to know the truth about his horse. A case for the authorities without a doubt. And Sidney Slyter says: my prognostications are always right. . . .

The cigarette burned in a saucer next to the brilliantine, and there was steam at the open lavatory door and sunlight at the raised window. Larry washed down to the muscles of his neck and arms, but the tips of his fingernails were black. He was whistling. Again he held the brushes in two hands, applied them simultaneously to the shine of his hair.

It was one o'clock, the racing crowd was at the Damps, and only the constable took a standing ale in the hotel's taproom while the wireless reported the condition of the horses. The foam was high on his tankard.

Larry whistled again, opened the bottom drawer, and from between layers of tissue lifted a vest of linked steel, shiny, weighing about five pounds. It fit over the undervest like silk. He turned sideways to adjust the ties. Then he carried a moist towel to the bathroom, finished his tea—it was bitter after the mouthwash and paste, and cleaner—and sat in the horsehair rocker in the sun by the window. He raised his black shoes to a footstool mauve and fringed with tassels, the sun began to glow against the steel beneath his shirt. He had changed the water in the flower vase first thing, so that was done; the pistol was loaded; he smelled fish frying in the kitchen next to the Tap. A small biplane was dragging a sign across the air in the direction of the spirited crowds: *Win with Wally*. He glanced at the yellow petals, a corner of his pillow, at Sparrow who was stretched on the bed. Then he nodded down at his black shoes, thick and perfect as parade boots.

"Put a little spit on them, Sparrow," he said, and watched the other climb off the bed, kneel, begin to polish.

Sparrow caught up with Larry near the Booter's. They walked by the steam baths—it had a marble front and, waist-high, two protruding and flaking iron pipes—walked by red petrol tanks, the beef posters, the hedgerow upon which the birds were hopping, a novelty shop with a rubber bride and groom in the window. On a low wooden door the single word *Jazz* was chalked and beside the door stood a pot of drying violets. Sparrow walked with the perspiration coming out on his chin; the sun flashed from his mother's wedding band on his pinky. Larry whistled and there was hardly a movement of the pale lips.

All about them was the stillness of the village: this watering place of cocaine and scent, beer and feather mattresses and the transient rooms of menservants, all deserted by sports and gypsies and platinum girls. Deserted except for the constable, themselves, and the captive in the white building. The small bets now—on a kiss, for show, for the cost of lunch, the small and foolish bets for fun—were being placed elsewhere along with the serious wagers for a sick wife, burial of an aged woman, relief from debt, a trip to the beach, and there were few risks in the village now except those taken by the telephone operator who made small business with anyone owning an instrument. The widow who had held Michael Banks' face in her hands at breakfast was sleeping when Larry and Sparrow started their day; the constable's lips were salty; the girl who had screamed was crying herself into dreams on the floor. But Larry and Sparrow were walking through the odor of old trees, through the village diaphanous and silent, walking now in search of Thick and Little Dora.

On the stair, carpeted with rubber held firm by tacks, smelling of varnish and the rubber, a dark stair yet safe, the two men stopped to light up thin cigarettes; then Larry went first and Sparrow followed. From the end of the second-floor hall came the sound of a flushing toilet, the sudden swift plash of water in pipes, and a moment later the tinkling of a key. Nothing more. The hall, tinted green, was without decoration, without furniture except for a steamer trunk with lid half-raised on ancient petticoats and a bottle of silver-coated pills.

When he pulled open the door the little girl darted past, but Sparrow snatched at her arm—she smelled of Paradise Shore, had her hair full of pins—and twisted her round to the room again. He could feel the sweet pith of her arm, the ordinary thinness of flesh without ruffles. Under his fingers was a vaccination still bandaged and the spot was warm, a bit of radiance on the skin which, since her day in the clinic, she had attempted to hide under her short sleeve.

"Where's Sybilline?" asked the child, but Sparrow said nothing, letting his hand touch the hair that made him shiver just to feel it, to feel the pins which the girl had found and a few which Little Dora had stuck into it from a cardboard for her amusement. He put his hand in his pocket.

"Syb wouldn't want you running off," he murmured.

Everyone stared at Larry: Sparrow and the child now, and the two women, Little Dora with her shadow of mustache, steel spectacles, purple hat in place, and the captive Margaret whom they had dressed only in a white shapeless gown tied behind with cords. And two men, Thick with his ear close to a portable radio, listening to the sounds of sport—if not of horses then dogs or cars or motorcycles—and on the opposite side of the room from him, suit dusty and smelling of straw, the trainer Cowles, enormous and seated on an upended valise, shirt unfastened and his hair raised into a nasty crust. All of them stared, and there was no dirt on Larry's collar. Now Larry was in the room, and even when drunk he could comport himself. But he was not drunk, was at the other extreme from the full bottle, cognac preferred, which it took to make him laugh. Stood straight as he did when predicting, Larry who was an angel if any angel ever had eyes like his or flesh like his.

"My God," said Little Dora, "you've been bathing again." Her chin twitched.

"Afternoon, Cowles," said Larry over her head, "afternoon, Miss. Are you comfortable?" And he nodded to Thick, who turned off the radio. "Well," after a moment, "there's something sweet in the air. Wouldn't you say so, Sparrow?"

But he was looking at Margaret, at the bare feet, the whiteness of the charity gown, the shoulders sloping in the big armchair. "Well, Miss, you haven't answered my question." He waited, and she was deprived of everything, stripped as for some dangerous surgery.

"I'm comfortable," she said, and leaned forward in the chair.

"You're not wanting then."

"No. They tell me I can't see Michael. . . ."

"That's true, Miss. You can't see Mr. Banks. Right, Cowles?"

"He's engaged," said the trainer and laughed, face and neck still damp with a horse's drinking water.

Margaret's brown skirt, the shoes, the stockings had been burned and it was Thick who had returned with the playing cards and white gown. Little Dora had held it for her—"You won't be going into public in this rig, it's open behind!"—then fastened the ties. Once they had cut into her cousin's abdomen and she recognized the gown: whenever Thick had the chance, he whispered how he had attended his mother in Guy's Hospital in order to see the young women on the wards. Now she was herself attended and was ashamed to move. Thick had burned her things, identification card and all.

Suddenly she looked at Cowles: "Do what you want with me. But leave Michael alone. . . ."

"Don't listen to him," said the child Monica, and pushed the little table in front of Margaret, sat opposite and dealt the cards. "Just play with me," she said, turning up a golden queen, "we're friends." She was wearing a bright-green dress, too short, and she drummed on one of her pointed knees while staring at the figure on the card. Monica had the redness of her mother's hair at the back of her neck. "I bet I've got a jack under here."

Sparrow's own knees were aching. After being ground beneath the treads of an armored vehicle, the bones and ligaments of his legs had shrunk, in casts had become dry and grafted together. His knee caps were of silver and it was the metal itself, he claimed, that hurt. Now at either corner of his mouth the skin turned suddenly white and Larry took a step, held him up by the arm. Then under the shoulders, under the knees, Larry lifted him—Sparrow dropped the beret—and carried him to the bed where the small man lay whimpering.

"Take off his shoes, Cowles. Carefully, if you please."

Cowles did as he was told, the dark coat flapping down over his hands at the laces, while the others—the radio was on the floor, a chair scraped—moved all together toward the bed. Sparrow, at such moments, was in the habit of shutting his eyes, whether instantly crippled in a picture palace, the Majesty, or in the Men's, whether caught in Daphne's Row or in the room with tables and dirty silverware. He was closing the lids now. They lowered, one or two lashes in each, slowly obliterating the eyes, which were white and without tears. A single lick of black hair lay on his forehead.

They were all at the bed, Thick and Larry on either side of the pillow with Little Dora and Cowles—he was still holding the empty shoes—and their expressions were unchanged even by Sparrow's moans. Margaret and the little girl came also, stood in the vicinity of Sparrow's heart and lungs.

From his great height, drawing back his coat flaps and lapels so that the gun and the gun's girdle—the holster, straps, strings—were visible, slowly putting his hands in his pockets, Larry spoke the name, Larry who had been the first to carry him the night he screamed, who had sipped tea out of a tin cup while watching them give preliminary treatment to the broken legs, and who had known immediately upon sight of the buttocks tiny and gnarled that the injured man was a rider: "Sparrow." And Larry, who had greased his hair even in battle, was still compassionate. "Sparrow," he said again and the moaning stopped, the perspiration appeared, the slit eyes began suddenly to tighten and grow shrewd.

"Dead and dying," came Sparrow's answering whisper at last, and the wrists twisted in the enormous cuffs.

"Now then, Thick," said Larry, "roll up his sleeve."

Sparrow grimaced and all the while kept the round vague outline of Margaret's face in his filmy sight. Larry took the tin packet from inside his coat, from just beneath the armpit's holster, and opened it. He fitted the needle to the syringe, broke the neck of the ampule, drew back the plunger until the scale on the glass measured the centimeters correctly. The tip of the needle dribbled a bit. He had tended to Sparrow in alleys, bathhouses with crabs and starfish dead on the floors, in doorways, in the Majesty, and the back of horsedrawn wagons on stormy nights. He had jabbed Sparrow in the depths of a barroom and upright in the booth of a phone; once on rough water with the rain beating down, once in a railway coach with his ministrations hidden from the old ladies behind a paper. Once too in the dark of a prison night, and many times, on leave, with some strange fat girl wearing rolled stockings, or with a tall girl carrying her underclothes in a respirator bag, standing idly by and swinging the bag, pulling the rolled elastic, watching. As often as Sparrow fainted, Larry revived him. Whenever Sparrow could stand on his feet no longer, whenever he went down in the crooked swoon, helpless as when he had first screamed from his bloody blankets—he had won a fiver from the kid of the battalion only that sundown—Larry the angel, the shoulder man, who later drowned the operator of the half-track in a shell hole filled with stagnant water and urine of the troops, took him up in his arms as carefully and coolly as a woman of long service. And with the needle and morphic fluid calmed him, standing then in suspect shadow, smoking, until Sparrow should rise, muttering, "Shivers and shakes," and proceed with his drugged and jittery step to a brief meal or to the job.

"This ought to do it," he said, and leaned forward, pinched as much of the flesh on Sparrow's arm as he could into a chilly blister. Then he punctured it, slid the needle beneath Sparrow's skin, gently pushed down the plunger. For a moment he could see the fluid lying like a pea just under the skin, then suddenly it dropped into a duct or into the mouth of a vein and was gone. He withdrew the needle and there was a tiny heart of blood on the tip of it. He watched, and in the middle of the tattoo—a headstone with "Flander's Field" in scroll beneath it—his pinch marks and the nick of the needle were still visible. He was casting a long shadow across Sparrow's torso, and the substance of his own head, the lines of his shoulders—constructed to catch a man's love for master tailoring—these lay lightly on the man in his agony. Then he looked across to Thick, who was stooping also and hiding his mouth behind a hand, keeping an eye on the bare needle. Thick's own forehead was trickling.

"He ain't going to need a transfusion . . . is he now, Larry?"

"Cover him with a sheet, for God's sake, and let's go," said Little Dora, and dug with mannish fingers into her stuffed side.

"Michael was sick once," whispered Margaret, and she was kneeling.

But this was not Sparrow's worst. Nor was it Daphne's Row or escaping in the manure wagon or trying to fix the needle behind the newspapers that time on the rocking train that had caused Larry himself to sweat and think of summoning the doctor who was bald and unlicensed and the best in the business for a man who had been stabbed or shot in the groin. None of these, but the time in the hock and antique shop—when the black cars passed up and down in front of the cluttered window and Sparrow had collapsed on a scabrous tiger skin, pulling a tea set with him and falling with his mouth jammed into the heel of a brass boot and he, Larry, had tried to squat beside and reach for him through a pile of bone and silken fans. His knee had crushed an old bellows and dust fell all about them, while paper weights rolled against the tiger's head. He had crouched there over Sparrow and had torn the tin packet. And a parrot in the back of the shop kept screaming, "Piss in his eye, piss in his eye!" from a great fortress-shaped wire cage. And while the cars hunted them up and down the street, while the parrot shrieked, he had freed Sparrow's arm from the cloth and had been too hasty, then, withdrawing the point, so that the needle broke, and the skin immediately turned blue. But even that day he had managed, watched Sparrow's cheekbones recede under a little color, helped him to crawl through the tunnel of Spanish shawls and so to escape, and had killed the parrot by stuffing his handkerchief into its shocked and gloomy face. Dragging Sparrow away he had heard the cage still swinging.

"That will do, I imagine," he said, and straightened. But no one else moved. First one, then by twos and threes the playing cards blew off the table and swished to the floor or landed on edge with tiny clacking noises, all face down except the queen. Thick wet his lips; Little Dora lifted back her veil; Cowles was biting his nails.

Monica blinked her green and fearful eyes and Sparrow from the bed was sighing.

"Better now, Sparrow? Come along then. . . ."

"Wait!" said Little Dora. "You don't mean you're going without me, Larry! You wouldn't leave Little Dora behind! Not another day in the Roost. And I thought I'd be out today and have a throw and a lunch at the Pavilion. Ain't I going to get a finger in the Golden Bowl at least? Or at least a look at the Bumpy Girl? What the hell, I'm no matron. . . ."

But Larry opened the door a crack. "She wants watching, Dora." And, bracing Sparrow, raising his head slightly: "Use the ropes if you need to, Thick."

The door closed and Margaret remained kneeling at the empty bed. Little Dora tore off her gloves. Thick began to laugh.

There was a railing and Michael Banks took hold of it, then stared down into the darkness of five broad swinging doors. He was quite alone when he pushed through one of them. Underneath the grandstand and at the bottom of the steps he found ahead of him the empty reaches of the public lavatory—low ceiling, fifty feet wide and of concrete painted black and tiny brick cubes washed with a light-green color. There were a few bulbs in cages waist high between the urinals and toilet bowls. It was the rank darkness of the empty Tube; a man could hide even at the base of one of those toilets if he crouched low enough, made himself small.

He started to whistle softly and the sound coming from his own lips—he was not often a whistler, a smiler—made the words "barrels of fun" go round in his head. Slowly he unbuttoned his coat and listened. He was standing, he noticed, near a toilet that had no seat, one badly defaced in the row of urinals. Once he had seen a man die on a toilet—from fear—then had found a notice of the death in the papers. "Why are you always reading obituaries?" He remembered that ugly voice. "Who do you expect to find on the lists?" He couldn't say.

Now he peered ahead at a row of pipes with great brass valves—he had never been able to turn taps beneath a sink, could not bring himself to touch the copper ball, slime-covered, gently breathing, that lay in the bottom of a toilet tank—thinking that it wouldn't do at all to walk down there.

Then he heard the footsteps. They were none he knew, not those of Lovely, Cowles, or the jockey, who had a light and bitter tread. These were the sounds of a measured step, the left foot heavier than the right, the dragging of shoe nails against the stones. And Banks saw a movement, a mere breaking of shadow, at the end of the tunnel by which he himself had entered. He turned, starting toward the opposite end where the pipes loomed, but there too he saw the flickering of a white hand, fragments of darkness about to become the shape of a man. So he wheeled close against the nearest urinal and clutched at his clothing.

The man was beside him. A man smaller than Banks, humped over, with feet large as boxes and a slate strapped across his chest. The name of a horse was on the slate: *Rock Castle.*

Banks kept his eyes forward, said nothing. But down the tunnel's opposite length, climbing from behind the pipes themselves, the shape of the second man became complete. And at his side, in silent metamorphosis, appeared the third. The hanging slate of the first man banged against Banks' hip, and that of the second—all these carried the little boards, buckles and leather, wood frames splintered, pieces of slate chalk-dusted—caught him on the opposite side under the ribs. And the second man's nearest rubber, several sizes too large, smacked in the latrine water, moved again and lay beside his own wet shoe. Banks held tightly to his clothes, heard them shuffle, breathe, splash loudly. They were just the three to stand beside him in the Men's—he knew it was inevitable with the first echo of the footsteps—just the sort to gang up on a lone man underground. But he also knew them for another kind: in the glare above, all along the track's inner rail, great numbers of these were posted, swiftly chalking, communicating with the crowd. Dressed in rags, lean, fast as birds. These were the men who sat on the rails with knees drawn up and scraps of paper fastened to their lapels, soothsayers with craftiness and eyes that never stopped. Very methodical. For days he had seen them, the jaws unshaved, the looks of intelligence, the slates slung like accordions from the worn-out straps. They were a system—"eunuchs," Cowles called them, "the mathematicians"—but while clacking within arm's length of the hoof-cut turf, each one sat in his astrological island, shabby, each figuring for himself with twitching cheek muscles and numbers scratched on the slate. "The bad-luck fellows," Cowles said of them.

Now Banks knew it to be so. The weight of the hands on the urinal, the thickly rubbered foot, the hat in the band of which was a photograph of a nude woman, the slates—the name *Rock Castle* was scrawled also on the other two—all this said as much.

And he was helpless now.

The first to come was whispering. Banks glanced quickly and saw a scar hanging down from the eye like a hair, saw spectacles and a loose soft collar partly torn at the seam. He tried to look away, but the man went on with his whispering.

"I've got a word for you: *Sybilline's in the Pavilion.* Do you understand? *Sybilline's in the Pavilion. . . .*"

Down and back the length of the latrine it was a false and cheerful sound. And behind the spectacles the man had watering eyes, eyes nearly awash in the sockets, and he did not blink. On either side of his nose—bookish—were grains of blood and scratches. When he whispered, the saliva behind his lips, between his teeth, was tinted pink with blood constantly trickling into the throat. The water round the eyes was clear. And his limpid sight, the smile, his whispering, the signs of struggle, the poverty of the cloth, his pink and golden gleam, the slate—these suggested unnatural occupation, the change in character: a man good for certain kinds of hire.

"Don't move now, Mr. Banks, not a move if you please."

There was no smile, only the single flaw, the perversion, the staring eyes and all round him the rank gloom, the chill, the burning of the rusty lights.

"It's three to one now, Banks. Don't take it into your head to run off in a scare."

This whisperer was on his right; the second to come stood patiently on his left; Polka-dots—there was a neckerchief round his throat—had moved up close behind him. It was the triangle of his dreams, the situation he dreaded at the sound of sirens. He wanted composure when the whisperer touched his arm, saying, "You won't dart then. That's sensible. Why look here, Banks," smiling again, reaching into a pocket behind the slate, "What do you make of these?" And in his palm, suddenly, he held two small black balls, sovereign-sized in diameter and perfectly round. They appeared soft, made of tar perhaps, and left an oily dark stain on the skin as the man shifted them in his hand. "Ever seen one of these before? Pellet bombs. Quite a charge in them, Banks. Not enormous of course, but good enough to take a foot or a hand or eye without any question. Should you scare, Banks, and be so fancy as to skip on us, I'd throw one at you. And it would bring you to the flagging. But here," guiding him by the arm, "we don't need to risk a blasting. You won't be likely to run if you're sitting down. Now will you?"

They stopped at the broken toilet and Banks sat on it as best he could. They were standing close to his knees, making wet sounds with their boots and rubbers beside him, and it was worse than the crowds. Even the constable could help, he thought.

"Wait," he was squatting, staring up, could hardly see their faces, "what do you want?"

And the whisperer: "We could bash your brains," sucking sharply, feet trampling his own, huddling round him. "But," more easily, "that's not it for now. Later perhaps. Larry said to keep an eye on you all right. But Banks," catching him by the throat, pressing down upon him and smiling, "just take my word for it: *Sybilline's in the Pavilion.* She wants you to know, Mr. Banks, she thinks you'll understand. . . ."

And these three dropped back with their hands ready, arms hooked out defensively, and like boys flashing in an empty courtyard turned suddenly and—far apart, shoes scraping and slates caught close—raced off swiftly and with terrible clatter in the direction of the swinging doors.

He sat bent over in the quietness he had been looking for. It was a green world and he heard no echoes; they did not toss back any of their pellet bombs after all. He remained there on the piece of battered lavatory equipment for an endless time, and his eyes were half-shut.

4

SIDNEY SLYTER SAYS

Marlowe's Pippet Favored by Majority . . .

Retired Jockey to Ride Rock Castle in the Golden . . .

Owner Insists that Mystery Horse Will Run . . .

The wind's out of Slyter now; the hat's on the back of Slyter's head, all right all right. . . . Anyone got a drink? Anyone got a consoling word? Five pounds for the reader who sends me a bit of helpful information. . . . Because I took half a day to drive to the Manor House and return (if you know the uncharted moors on a summer day you know how desperately your Slyter drove). Arrived in time for tea—the little black cup you always suspect of being poisoned—and Lady Harvey-Harrow sent down to the empty stables for poor old Crawley. He came after a while, brushing through the cobwebs and removing his cap, and Lady Harvey-Harrow looked at him and said I was a gentleman from the Press. Still looking at him—mind you, not once my way—she asked him whether or not he agreed that the horse was dead, saying that it was her impression that the horse was dead but that if by chance the animal was still alive why those who had carried him off were welcome to such an old and useless horse. "What about it, now," I said, "dead or alive?" And the old man leaned over and stared hard as he could into Lady Harvey-Harrow's eyes and said—no more than a whisper—said that he had changed his mind and recollected having seen the horse not a fortnight ago in a shaded and gloomy place beneath the lone oak tree—the lightening tree he said—beside the river separating her Ladyship's heath from Lord Henry's land, and he remembered thinking how poorly the horse was looking at the time. I took up my hat and the old woman said she would not pursue the matter and suggested that I do the same. . . . How's that for a story to tell an established journalist? So Sidney Slyter's had it—for the moment—and Mrs. Laval is not in her accustomed room tonight. Unsatisfactory. But I'll get our men to check the files, that's what I'll do. . . .

How many are going to St. Ives?

Lines of people filed among the tables in the Pavilion, long lines wound between the little metal folding chairs all taken. They were coming down from the stands, from the stable area, from amusement tents, tramping across the beds of flowers left crushed or covered with spittle. White faces, a hat or two, a hearing aid, all packed together, stranger against stranger, and making their voices shrill over winnings or poor luck. The weight of them tipped a table up now and then, and spoons, forks with pastry on the tips, glassware, slid and fell from the edge. Those seated at the tables tried to drink, eat, talk, but everyone in the queues was laughing, stood staring down at the little round metal tops and puddles of lemonade and burned matches. There was a fat woman who carried her own sweets in a bag, and a cream puff had exploded against her cheek leaving bits of chocolate and egg white on her rosy skin. She was laughing from a deep stomach and dabbing with a fistful of handkerchief.

With the bottom of his trousers wet, brown hat on the back of his head, shirt crumpled and pinched lips smashed together, there was no happiness of the throng for Michael Banks, and he struck out at an elbow, at a shoulder blade, as hard as he dared. He saw the young woman immediately and gave a whistle. But it was drowned in the noise and upset of a waiter's tray.

She had a table to herself and had saved him a seat. She was drinking pink water and gin out of a tall glass and there was a second pink glass for him on the scratched metal table edge before his chair. A giant pair of binoculars lay between her glass and his and the long strap was bound safely round her wrist. Her red hair was like the orange of an African bird, and when she sipped, the jockey-pink rose water sent a delicate color up to a row of tiny pearls which she had sunk into the deepness of the hair.

"I'm Sybilline," she said.

He looked at the tip of her tongue and smelled the gin. Suddenly in the midst of weak eyes, puffy shirts, wallets stuffed with photographs of dead mothers and home, and on his person carrying still the clamminess, he found himself thinking he could bear the crowds for this, and felt his feet dragging, his fingers pressing white against the sticky metal of the chair. Yet he was brief.

"You wanted a word with me?"

"Oh, come off it now," she laughed. "Sit down and have a drink with Sybilline."

He did not remove his hat. He kept his back straight and with both hands seized the frosted glass, drank heavily. Everyone else wanted fish and chips or onions, but the gin and pink water was enough for him. There were fine soft flaming hairs on the woman's arms, freckles like little brown crystals out of the sea. The sun struck through the canvas and lighted her, here in the midst of a crowd which lifted his chair then allowed it again to settle. He hung on, swallowed, watched the way she breathed—there were holes cut in the tips of her brassière—and the way her fingers always curved round her windpipe when she brought her free hand to her throat. She was thin if anything and her skin was white as if it had taken all the skin's pigmentation, flesh color, to tint the hair.

"What did you want of me then?" he asked, and the chair was inching about beneath him, man and chair pressed into motion by the crowd on the Ouija board of the Pavilion's floor.

And quickly, brightening up: "I'm here for the weekend only and, fancy now, there's you! I've had a look through these," raising the strap of the binoculars, "and the fellow who owns them is gone. Aren't you glad?

Things just come to pass, for a girl. For you, too, if you can only manage a little cheer in your face! Here, you carry them."

Slowly he put the strap over his shoulder. "But I haven't heard of you before," he said, and let the cold glass click against his teeth.

A small narrow man, appearing drunk and soldierly and wearing a red beret over an ear like a twist of leather, stumbled out of the queue and flung his arm round the woman's shoulder, shoved his cheek against the woman's cheek so that Banks saw the two heads together, the fair skin with its emulsion of cream and the scrap of the fellow's jaw, the green eyes meant for a mirror and the other eyes good only for sighting at a game of darts, the little red beret crushed into the softness of her orange hair. The man's breath stirred the pinkish curls and his short fingers were biting into the plain cloth above her breast. He was stooping, hugging her for balance, and Banks watched the two pairs of eyes, the twitching when movement came finally to the intruder's lips:

"Catch her while you can, Tosh," staring then, taking a breath too big for him, as if he himself had nobody in the world. "Stairways and stars, remember!" And Sybilline laughed, and with a hand on the man's thigh pushed him off so that he ducked quickly into the crowd.

Only her own eyes were left and Banks could not frown at them. "I'm a married man," he said. But there was a waltz coming out of the speaker, and she was laughing, twisting a curl the color of nail polish round her finger.

When they stood up, binoculars falling now against his hip, the fat woman and three others began fighting for the chairs, and his glass, still half-filled with gin, toppled and splashed on anonymous shoes and socks dropped carelessly below the ankles. But already Sybilline had him by the hand and Larry watched them going off through the crowd.

So Little Dora was left alone with Margaret. And Thick, driving the black van that had oil and sand smeared over the hand-painted name, was sent with Sparrow to the flat in the street at Dreary Station. Sparrow was agile now, climbed down from the cab and walked easily with the suitcase in his hand. Thick was grinning because he always liked a smashing. The sun lighted up the window boxes and the face of an old dog behind a fence; from far-off came the sounds of all the girls sewing in the factories.

"Gas johnnys," Sparrow told Mrs. Stickley and went with Thick to the flat and bolted the door from the inside. They took out the tools of the trade and in half an hour shredded the plant that the cat had soiled, broke the china quietly in a towel, stripped linen from the bed and all clothing out of the cupboards and drawers and closets, drank from the bottle found with the duster and pail. They cut the stuffing in bulky sawdust layers away from the frames of the furniture, gutted the mattress.

The high bells were ringing and Sparrow and Thick were done sawing the wood of the furniture into handy lengths, in sheeted bundles had carried out to the van the wood and the pieces of lingerie and puffy debris of their work. Bare walls, bare floors, four empty rooms containing no scrap of paper, no figured piece of jewelry or elastic garment, no handwriting specimen by which the identity of the former occupants could be known: it was a good job, a real smashing; and at dusk, on a heath just twenty miles from Aldington, they stopped and dumped the contents of the van into a quagmire round which the frogs were croaking. The two men smoked cigarettes in the gloom and then drove on.

Sybilline had let go of his hand and for a moment he did not lose her, stepping closely behind her figure, her red hair, quite certain she was lovely, even down to the open shoes and bare heels more red and wrinkled than he expected. But then the sound of a young woman's flat voice made him think of home, of Margaret; somebody knocked him in the side; and when he turned round again and discovered that Sybilline was gone he did not care. He was thinking of his wife Margaret and for the next hours fought alone through the crowd, thinking of her and sweating and becoming hungry.

And now, directly in front of the stands and just out of its shadow—above him was the tower with the gilded face of the clock hung over with canvas and a scaffold's few swinging timbers—standing in one of the crowd's brief islands of space, he put a sandwich of hard salted bread and cheese to his teeth and chewed quickly. Others were sitting: a few women with their legs out straight on dirty towels or a folded sweater; a man wearing a tall gray coachman's hat with enormous red and green tickets sticking out of the band and now resting himself in an armchair, an overstuffed chair tonic-stained and running on makeshift wheels; a boy lying out on his back and asleep. But Banks, though breathing quickly and sweating, preferred to stand. He kept the cheese close to his mouth, bit into the bread. His long shadow was taking food.

"Buy a ticket," mumbled the man from his chair. In weariness and the heat he sought Banks' eyes but was too overcome to move. Banks turned a little and his shadow, like the arm of a sundial, pointed at someone else. He had found his air hole, a bit of room for his feet, and no one was at his elbow, nobody crowded. For once there was not a familiar face in sight, Margaret would wait. No longer did he care about the roses in the green behind him, but kept his eyes on the sandwich.

"He don't need a ticket. Can't you see?" One of the women, young, alone, with small carbon-black pock holes covering her face, sitting with her skirts out of place on the dirty incline of the clay spread before the stands, tore slowly into little pieces her own ticket, a dare that had failed, and glanced at the man in the chair. "He don't need your kind of luck, our kind of luck. Can't you see? God, what a thirst I've got!"

And ignoring her: "Buy a ticket," the man said again, and the wheels squeaked for a moment.

"God," the woman continued, and looked once at the sky, "they ought to shoot that Islam. Say," talking not to the prostrate man but to Banks, "you didn't bet on

Islam, did you, mister? You'd know better, you would. He's broke my heart, that Islam. Say," he could feel a quickening of thought, a change in her eyes, "you wouldn't have a quid on you, mister?"

And quickly: "Watch out for her," the man said with an angry spinning of the wheels.

But Banks didn't care. He heard the voices of the man and girl—they were ringed round him and the bodies curtained out all except a far-off anonymous noise from the crowd—and he recognized the spent effort of the seller's voice and the appeal of the girl's. A little powder case was lying on its side next to her hip. But he had had enough of them and he was eating cheese.

"Here, I'll give you a quid," said a fat woman who was watching four or five chocolates melt in the palm of her hand.

The clay under his feet had grown hard with the spittle and rain, the sun, the endless weight of their bodies. It gave off an odor—of shoe leather, shredded tobacco, sweat. The sun was shining off their flesh. He moved his sundial's shadow again and peered at his teeth marks in the cheese; it made a dry bulb in his mouth and only the girl's remark about thirst had caught his attention. What if he showed her a pink lemonade and gin right now? She'd forget her Islam soon enough.

"Have one of my chocolates," said the woman.

He would watch out for all of them, he thought. Suppose he swallowed and looked at them, then said one word simply and clearly. What if he said "Larry"? The fellow in the chair would jump, most likely. But he buried the name, forgot it, thrust his face into the cheese which had no smell. He had never liked to stand while eating. Now he was grateful for the pause, the chance to stand apart though they were watching. Perhaps only the boy asleep was better off—no clock, no time, no witnesses for him. The face was bruised, bore the impression of knuckles beneath one eye. He would start, sit up, begin to cry if he heard the name of Larry, right enough.

Banks crumpled the sandwich paper and thrust it into his pocket.

"He's not so lucky," said the woman with chocolates, "he's only a kid." And she was looking at him squarely and he at her, and she had a man's thick lips, an arm she might throw about anyone's shoulder. "Tell us now," she said. "Are you the lucky boy? Have you been winning?"

He tried to look away. Then calmly, feeling the sun's pool hot in the top of his hat: "I've been picking them all correctly. But not for cash. . . ."

"You see," she shouted, "he hasn't got a quid!" And while laughing she licked the sweets, pulled a scrap of handkerchief from her skirt and began wiping the sticky palm. Her laughter awoke the boy and he groaned.

The girl laughed also, but less heartily, as if she might still hope to get what he did have.

"Shut up," said the man in the chair, "he's got more than that."

And over the heads of all those standing behind them, he saw the profile of Margaret's face. When he jumped, took the first long stride, he kicked something under his foot and in a moment knew it to be the young woman's powder case, without looking down, heard the tinkle and scrape of the contents scattering.

"Here, don't be rude. . . ," he heard the older woman say, and he was pushing, pushing away into the midst of them. And still there was the face and he gasped, slipped between two men in black, tried not to lose her, raised a hand. Here was surprise and familiarity, not out of fear, but fondness, and between them both perhaps three hundred others not moving, not caring what they lost in the sun.

"My God, what have they done to Margaret!" Because, for the moment only he saw the whole of her and she was wearing clothes he had never seen before—an enormous flower hat and a taffy-colored gown with black-beaded tassels sewn about the waist and sewn also just above the bottom that was dragging. A dress from another age, too large, too old, Margaret clothed in an old tan garden gown and lost. "She's not yet thirty," he thought, shoving, using his elbow, "where's their decency?" Then she was gone and he shouted.

"Watch who you're colliding with, young cock," said a voice in his ear.

He reached the spot where she had stood, but only a man, somebody's butler, with a small child on his shoulders, moved in her place now, and the man refused to talk. The child looked down at Banks.

So he turned, stumbled, and near the east corner of the stand saw the last of the taffy back rushing like the ghost of a doe, and they were hustling her—another woman and a man. "Wait!" he was only thinking it, "wait!" Here was the first taste from the cup of panic, seeing the girl, his wife, pulled suddenly away from him by an arm. When he reached the spot he found that Margaret had been caught at the top of the stairs leading down to the five swinging doors of the Men's, and he stopped, drew back, put his hand on the rail. A cigarette flung in anger, haste, was burning down there near one of the vaulted doors and he thought he could hear still the old public squeak of the hinge. He could not descend those stairs, and once more he was tasting lime. In the cool shadow he leaned, clutched the dusty iron, closed his eyes.

"Mr. Banks." It was Cowles, accompanied by Needles dressed in his silks. "Why, Mr. Banks, you'd better take care in the sun. Ain't that right, Jimmy?"

"I saw her. . . ," he managed to say.

"Who's that, Mr. Banks?"

"I saw my wife. . . ."

"Well, too bad for that, Mr. Banks, as the fellow says. Ain't that right, Jimmy?"

"They took her into the Men's."

"Unlikely, I should say. You'd better watch the sun, Mr. Banks. Come now," and he could hear the jockey shuffling his little boots, "come, you'd better join us at the Baths. They're bracing, Mr. Banks, very bracing. . . ."

"Fool," shaking the white gown in his face, "you fool!"

"But she pilfered the trunk, I tell you."

"I never let it happen . . . but you did. You fool!"

"And what's so smart about having a trunk full of clothes in the hall when you're trying to keep her naked?"

"Don't say smart to me, smart as a naked girl, you are! And I can't even take a slip to watch the Bumpy Girl without you letting her at a trunk full of clothes that would keep us all in style."

"You wasn't supposed to be taking a slip. You was supposed to stay."

"Don't throw it back at me, don't give us that! Just wait 'til Larry hears how it was you who was lax, you wait. . . ."

"Ah, Dora, I can't keep awake all day."

5

SIDNEY SLYTER SAYS

Mystery Horse's Odds Rise Suddenly . . .

Rock Castle's Trainer Suffers Gangman's Death . . .

Marlowe's Pippet: The Youngster Can Scoot . . .

. . . my great pleasure in announcing that I have sent five pounds, as promised, to one Mr. Harry Bailey, Poor Petitioners, Cock & Crown, East End. Mr. Bailey, carter by trade, suggests that, in his own words, "The horse will win. Ain't it the obvious fact which the old woman and her old groom are hidin'? My poor lame sister dreamt it now three nights in a row, that the horse will win. And all respects, Mr. Slyter, I'm of the opinion she's exactly right." There's a tip to make Sidney Slyter quake, there's one for your pals! Dead, alive, uncertain of age, uncertain of origin, suspected ownership—victory these things say to our reader in East End! Perhaps you've put your finger on it, Mr. Bailey—the simple conviction of your phrasing chills my heart, Mr. Bailey, with the suffering which our ancients knew—but we must not blaspheme the outcome of the Golden Bowl with such ideas of

> certainty. What have the rest of you to say? Anyhow, congratulations to Mr. Bailey, cheers to Mr. Bailey's sister. And five pounds to the next lucky person writing in. . . . But it's Sidney Slyter here, and my assistant Eddie has been put on the job of checking our files. Eddie will be checking them now and, any moment now, will be calling me direct from Russell Square. Eddie's just the boy for checking files. . . . And this is a new development: officials here have made it known that T. Cowles, of undesirable character and listed as trainer of Rock Castle, has been stabbed to death by members of a gang to which the victim Cowles himself belonged. And Sidney Slyter says queer company for Mr. Banks? Queer and dangerous? Fellow who operates the lift said Mrs. Laval was not available tonight; stepped out for dancing and bitters with a friend, he said. So Sidney can sit in the pub with the constable, or go throw dirty dice in the lane. But cheer up, cheer up, Eddie will be through to your Sidney Slyter soon. . . .

Michael Banks and Cowles and the jockey in his colors walked past the Booter's, past the barn and millinery shops until they reached the Baths, where they found the constable's two-wheeler leaning against the marble wall with water dripping from one of the iron pipes down to its greasy seat. A few bees were circling the klaxon and the water made a rusty summer's pool on the leather.

"Look out," said Cowles, "the old constable's after his cleanliness again."

"He's been drinking," the jockey said. "He wants to sweat away the beer. That's all."

The entrance to the Baths was on an alley. The building was of whitewashed stone and marble, and once, years before, the entire alley side had served as a sign. Now on the dirty white the paint was faded, but most of the letters in gold and brown could still be read: across the top of the wall and in a scroll "Steam Bathing" and under that the words "Good for Gentlemen," and then another slogan, "Steam Cleans and Cures." On either side of the door was painted the greater-than-life-size figure of a naked man, one view seen from the front, the other from the rear, both flexing their arms and both losing the deep red flesh of their paint to the sun and weather of harsh seasons.

Banks smiled once when he walked naked from the dressing room into the steam. He was immediately hot, wet in an instant, and felt his way through the whiteness that was solid and rolling and solid again all at once. Now and then four or five square feet would clear completely, and in one of these sudden evaporations he saw Cowles standing quite still and stretching, while the jockey was taking blind tentative steps, covering his face and mouth with the fingers and thumbs. But he heard the hissing, the sightlessness returned; they were groping in the same direction. Then: "Here, Mr. Banks," it was Cowles, obliterated but close to him in the steam, "lie here. There's room for three of us right here."

There were tables—three now pushed together—tables and shelves to lie upon, slippery and warm, and a collection of live red iron pipes upon which the Steam Baths operator and his two young boys threw buckets of icy water: and the steam smelled first of flame, cold mountain streams, and of the bare feet and ankles of the man and boys at work. And then it smelled of wood, stone floors, of white lime sprinkled between the slats on the stone; and of the bathers then, the molecules of hair oil and sweat from the skin. He breathed—and tasted, smelled the vapors filling the lung, the eye, the ear. So many clouds of it, so thick that the tin-sheeted walls were gone and only a lower world of turning and crawling and groaning men remained.

The shelving, wide enough for a man, was built about the room in tiers that reached nearly to the ceiling, all this space cut by braces, planks, verticals. Between the tiers were the tables with hands, feet, at the edges. It was a crowded ventless chamber and filled with noise, a confused and fearful roaring. But these men were prone and here activity was nothing more than a turning over or a writhing. Every few minutes the smallest of the two boys would fling a pail of ice water not on the pipes but across the flesh of a prostrate bather and the man would scream: no place here for undervests or socks, tie clasp or an address written out on paper.

". . . Lie next to me, Mr. Banks," and Cowles helped him up to the boards while the jockey climbed as best he could. Then the three of them were stretched out together and he felt that he himself was smiling. There was slime on the wood and steam was dripping down the braces, down the legs of soaking pine. By habit he started on his back and kept his hands at his sides, restraining his hands even when he felt the eyelids turning soft and his lips loosening, taking the seepage in. He heard the splashing of ice water but it was aisles away, and the steam was heaped up all about him, his lungs were hot. Then, later, he listened to Cowles succumbing, the flesh —a hand or foot—beating against the wood and growing still, the moans filled with resistance, helplessness, and finally relief as if confessing under the blows of a truncheon.

". . . Makes you feel . . . like . . . you'll never walk again . . . eh, Mr. Banks?" Now a whisper only and the head buried down under the fatty arms, one huge leg fallen over the edge, never to be retrieved.

Banks rolled over, making the effort to throw off the pinion and move despite the nervelessness of muscles, despite paralysis. "Excuse me, Needles," he said, but the jockey had his own discomfort and did not reply.

He always saved the stomach. It was best on the stomach and he waited until just that moment before he might not be able to roll at all, then tried it, and the exertion, the slickness of wood passing beneath his skin, the trembling of the propped arm—when these were gone there came the pleasure of shoulders sagging, of being face down in the Baths. Now he opened his eyes a little and his lips parted around the tongue. He thought of water to drink. Or lemonade. Or gin. He knew the torpor now, the thirst, with all the fluids of his body come to the surface and the hair sticking closely to his skull.

And then—not able to raise his head, drifting back from numbness and feeling the rivulets sliding down his flesh—he heard the sounds, the voices, that had no business in the Baths: not the steam's hissing nor the groans of bathers, but the swift hard sounds of voices just off the street.

". . . Gander at that far corner, if you please, Sparrow. And you, Thick, shadow the walls."

Moments later, back through the oppression: "Go down on your knees if you have to, Sparrow. . . ."

And the steam lay on the body of Jimmy Needles, and Cowles looked dead away. He thought he saw shadows through the puffs and billowing of the whiteness and he longed more than anything for a towel, a scrap of cloth to clutch to himself, to wipe against his eyes. In the anonymity of the Baths, amidst all those naked and asleep, he heard again the sounds and now he tried to rouse the trainer: "Cowles," whispering, "Come awake now, Cowles."

But then there was the ice blow of the water, and he heard the grunt of the child and pail's ring even before the sharp splash covered him from head to foot. He froze that moment and the skin of his shoulders, legs, back and buttocks pained with the weight of the cold more shocking than a flame. When he bolted upright, finished wiping the water from his eyes, he found that Cowles was gone and in a glance saw nothing of Needles except a small hand losing hold of the flat boards as the jockey shimmied down and away.

So he followed and several times called out: "Cowles, Cowles!" But he got no answer. He crouched and crept down the length of one wall, made his way in blindness and with the floor slats cutting into his feet. He moved toward the center and was guided by the edges of the tables.

And then there were three separate holes in the steam clouds and in one he saw the stooping figure of the man with the beret; in another he saw Thick scratching his chin; and in the last, the nearest, the broad tall body of Larry fully dressed, and his dark-blue suit was a mass of porous serge wrinkled and wet as a blotter. The cloth hung down with steam. The shirt, at collar, cuffs, and across the chest, was transparent as a woman's damp chemise and the chest was steel. He carried a useless handkerchief and the red was quickly fading from his tie, dripping down over the silken steel. Thick was wearing a little black hat that dripped from the brim, and Sparrow's battle trousers were heavy with the water of the Baths.

Banks squatted suddenly, then spoke: "What are you after now? Three beggars, isn't it?"

Without answering or looking down at him the men began to fade. Not gone suddenly behind the vapor's thick intrusion, but merely becoming pale, more pale as shred by shred the whiteness accumulated in the holes where they stood. A sleeve, a hand, the tall man's torso, a pair of wet shoes—these disappeared until nothing was left of the trio which, out of sight, continued then the business of hunting despite the steam.

"Go on," he heard himself saying, "go on, you bloody beggars. . . ."

Slowly he crawled under the braces of the table and

after them. The steam was heavy and his eyes began to smart. He tore his calf on a splinter. Once more, and for the last time in the Baths, he came upon the toe of Larry's black boot, followed the trouser leg upwards to the lapel where a yellow flower was coming apart like tissue, saw the crumpled handkerchief thrust in his collar, the sheen of perspiration on the high cheeks, the drops of water collected around the eyes. But still there was the casual lean to the shoulders, one hand in one wet pocket as if he had nothing better to do than direct this stalking through a hundred and ten degrees and great dunes of steam. The boot moved, turned on the toe leather so that he saw the heel neatly strengthened by a bit of cobbler's brass, and the man was gone again, saying: ". . . Found him, Thick? Have a go under the steam pipes then."

And he himself was creeping off again, feeling his foot drag through a limpid pool, feeling the sediment on his skin. His hair was paste smeared across his scalp. He felt how naked he was, how helpless.

Then, still on all fours, he came to the corner. Under the wooden shelving, lying half-turned against a stretch of soapstone, bent nearly double at the angle of meeting walls, crowded into this position on the floor of the Baths was Cowles' body with the throat cut. Banks crept up to him and stared and the trainer was a heap of glistening fat and on one puffy shoulder was a little black mole, growing still, Banks realized, though the man was dead. And though this Cowles—he had had his own kill once, kept dirty rooms in a tower in the college's oldest quad, had done for the proctor with a fire iron and then, at 4 A.M., still wearing the gown darned like worn-out socks, had stolen the shallow punt half-filled with the river's waters and, crouched heavily in the stern with the black skirts collected in his lap, had poled off under the weeping willow trees and away, lonely, at rest, listening to the fiends sighing in nearby ponds and marshes—though this Cowles now lay dead himself his blood still ran, hot and swift and black. His throat was womanly white and fiercely slit and the blood poured out. It was coming down over the collar bone, and above the wound the face was drained and slick with its covering of steam. One hand clutched the belly as if they had attacked him there and not in the neck at all.

Just as Banks caught the lime rising at the odor of Cowles' blood he felt flesh striking against his flesh, felt a little rush of air, and Jimmy Needles lunged at him in passing and fled, hunting for the door. Before he himself could move he heard a sound from the wood above Cowles' corpse, glanced up, and peered for several moments into the congealed blue-tinted face of the constable: an old man's naked face reflecting cow and countryside, pint-froth and thatch in all the hard flat places of its shape.

"Here now, what's this deviltry. . . ."

But then Banks too was gone, no longer crawling but running, with the unhelmeted head of the constable and the sight of Cowles' freshly cut throat before him, reaching the door as he heard the hiss and exhalation of new blinding steam and the cry of the old nude member, only member, of the constabulary showered that moment from the small boy's icy pail.

His hand slipped on the knob but it shut finally against the pushing of the steam, and the jockey handed him a towel. He covered himself, leaned back, stared at the bench upon which, shoulder to shoulder, were seated the three of them—Sparrow and Thick and Larry—with pools at their feet. Banks held the towel with both hands under the chin, looked at the dark men on the bench and the row of clothes hooks curling from the wall behind them. There was water about his own feet now.

"What did you kill him for?" Watching Larry in the middle but seeing the silks fluttering over the hump at the peak of the jockey's spine: "Whatever for?" It was little more than a whisper above which he could hear the water falling from three pairs of hands, dropping from three sets of trouser cuffs. The flower had disappeared altogether from the blue lapel.

"Oh, come on," said Sparrow, getting up, wringing the beret, "let's have a dash to Spumoni's!"

In the dusk surrounding the Baths the bees swarmed straight off the klaxon and made a golden thread from the bicycle to a nearby shrouded tree.

It seemed hardly more than teatime but it was dusk, fast coming on to nightfall when there's a fluttering in steeples and the hedgerow turns lavender, when lamps are lit on ancient taxis and the men are parading slowly in the yards of jails. Castles, cottages and jails, a country preparing for night, and time to set out the shabbiness for the day to come, time for a drink.

Sparrow felt the mood: "Give us another liter of that Itie stuff," he said. The waiter filled their glasses and Larry heaped the plates with second servings of the spaghetti and tomato sauce. The waiter could see the blue butt and shoulder holster inside his coat. "Cheers," said Sparrow, while Jimmy Needles drank his health.

And between the tables: "You dance divine," said Sybilline, "just divine. . . ."

A quartet of scar-faced Negroes was playing something Banks had first heard out of gramophones in Violet Lane, something whistled by the factory girls on their way to work. No favorite now, no waltz carried on the tones of an old cornet, but music that set him trying to pump Syb's hand up and down in time with the piano player's tapping shoe. There was a trumpet, a marimba and bass and the piano on which a white girl was supposed to sit and sing. Beside his bench was a flabby fern in a bucket and the piano player kept a bottle there, under the dead green leaves. Banks could clearly hear the fellow's foot going above the syncopation of the racy song.

Banks had never learned to dance but he was dancing now. He pumped her hand and Syb wasn't afraid to move, wasn't afraid to laugh, and he found her spangled slippers everywhere he stepped and saw the drops of candlelight—on the tables there were candles fixed to the bottoms of inverted tumblers—swelling the tiny pearls pushed into the fiery hair. For a moment, admiring the decorative row of pearls, he thought of the faces children model out of bread dough and of the eyes they fashion by sinking raisins into the dough with their stubby thumbs. Then, with the hand on her waist, he felt a bit of Sybilline's blouse pulling out of her skirt and heard her voice, flitting everywhere fast as her feet, saying, "Let's have a drink-up, Mike, a rum and a toss. . . ."

The room was filled with people from the Damps—a racing crowd. In this room in the town surrounded by farm and vicarage and throaty nightingale there were people who did their banking in High Fleet Seven and others who did their figuring in the slums, all sporting now—it was the night before the running of the Golden—and ordering Spumoni's best. Like a theater crowd, a society in which the small person of Needles could go unnoticed, though wearing rainbow silks and cap and a numbered placard on his puffy sleeve. And Banks felt that he too went unnoticed, felt that he could drink and dance and breathe unobserved at last. There were enormous black-and-white paintings of horses about the walls, along with the penciled handwritten names of endless guests. There was the odor of whisky and Italian cooking, and the Negroes never ceased their melody of love and Lambeth Walk.

"Coo, Mike," she said just before they reached the table, "it's going to be a jolly evening." In Syb's voice he heard laughter, motor cars and lovely moonlit trees, beds and silk stockings in the middle of the floor.

Glasses in hand they did not sit, but stood beside the table, because she wanted to dance again and couldn't bear sitting down. They held hands while the small ex-soldier poured and Needles sucked in his cigarette and looked up at him.

"Mr. Banks," and it was Larry, lifting the fork, letting the candle shine across his face, "feeling a little better now?"

"Quite nicely, thanks," he answered.

"Bottom's up!" the girl said suddenly, and swallowed off the wine, balancing against his arm and tilting so that he saw the heart throb, the wine's passage down the throat from which she was capable of laughing, crying, whispering. So he drank also and it was the hard dry dusty taste of wine and he was warmed and pleasurably composed. He remembered not the Baths, the Damps, poor wretched Cowles, nor the rooms in Dreary Station, but a love note he had written at the age of twelve when the city was on fire. And remembering it he looked at Sybilline and saw in her eyes the eyes of an animal that has seen a lantern swinging on a blackened hill.

"Excuse us," he said, and put down the glass. "This is our melody."

In his arms she was like the women he had thought of coming out of comfort rooms. Or it was what they had done in the shelters or when the bands were marching—upright, holding each other close before the parting. One of his hands was on her body and the sequins kept falling off her blouse to the floor. They were dancing on sequins. He was able now, while holding her, to try and tuck in the blouse.

"It's shrunk," she murmured, "it'll never stay." But

his fingers pushed in the cloth, and over the top of her auburn head he saw the piano player leaning to drink from the bottle pulled out of the bucket and saw the marimba player's black dusty hands—there was a big gold wedding band on one finger—shaking, trembling in mid-air. Everyone was talking horses, talking the Golden, but he was moving round the little floor with Syb.

"You know," pulling her head away from his brown lapels, but dancing, dancing, "that other chap was hopeless. Wouldn't even buy me an ice. But whatever did you do with his binoculars?"

He waited and then: "Gave them to a fellow selling tickets."

Later still, when she happened to see the jockey holding his head and Sparrow slipping something to the waiter—a Neapolitan with dirty shirt and mustaches—when the candles were softly dying and the wine was dregs—and still they were turning on the floor—then she laughed, spoke against his chest: "It'll be a jolly evening, Mike. I promise. We'll go to bed and you'll like my bed, Michael. . . ." And then in the middle of the floor with the others watching and Larry pulling sharply on his coat over the holster, sending Needles out for the hired car, then she gave him her own lips soft, venereal, sweet and tasting of sex.

But Sparrow stopped them kissing, tapped on his arm. "Come now, Banks, Larry says we're going to a proper place."

6

SIDNEY SLYTER SAYS

Marlowe's Pippet Smart in Practice Whirls . . .

Rock Castle Proves Ancient Champion . . .

Mystery Horse Possesses Danish Blood . . .

Harry Bailey of Poor Petitioners, Cock & Crown, East End, how right you were! Fly up to Aldington, Mr. Bailey, fly to Aldington with your poor lame sister, for Sidney Slyter says he needs you now! Five pounds? Not half enough, I'd say! Sidney—God's silent servant—Sidney Slyter has his brimming glass, his fags, lighter embossed with crop and stirrup, his hotel beds, and ladies to converse with in the bars; has his hard sporting eyes red-rimmed or not and under his titfor leaves of information about the horses ever growing bone from bone and blood into blood. And Sidney Slyter's got God's own careless multitude to shelter in enjoyment and the luck of sport. But Mr. Bailey, my friend, it took you puzzling over the problem while rubbing your dog's worn ear and hearing the dreams of your ever-innocent lame partner to perceive directly the horror at the end of our journey, you to phrase the spoils of our fate! *The horse will win . . . the horse will win. . . .* Amazing, Mr. Bailey, just amazing. . . . Because Eddie Reeves came ringing through my wires at 4 A.M. and what he read me was an accolade proper for the obituary of the King of the Turf: *He's run the Golden before, Sidney. Hear me Sidney? Entered in The Golden Bowl three times and three times the winner. Hear me Sidney?* Then the dates; then Eddie coughing through the dawn; then the minutes of each winning race. Then reading on: *Draftsman by Emperor's Hand out of Shallow Draft by Amulet; Castle Churl by Draftsman out of Likely Castle by Cold Masonry; Rock Castle by Castle Churl out of Words on Rock by Plebeian—Bred by the Prince of Denmark, Sidney, bred by the Prince and commanded to win by the Prince and ordained to win by the Prince and forebears of that line, too. And by his order—just to get the royal stamp on him, Sidney—the King's own surgeon transplanted a bone fragment from the skull of Emperor's Hand into Rock Castle's skull. Then presented by the Prince of Denmark to Lady Harvey-Harrow on her sixteenth birthday. The horse will win, Sidney, the horse will win. . . .* Rigid; fixed; a prison of heritage in the victorious form; the gray shape that forever rages out round the ring of painted horses with the band music piping and clacking; indomitable. And somebody knew all this already, and it wasn't Mr. Banks. But who? Sidney Slyter wants to know: and Sidney Slyter wants to know what's the matter with Mr. Michael Banks. . . .

It was 4 A.M. in the darkness that had begun with bees and warbling and the fading of bells, and Thick had used the ropes. Now she was bound, her wrists were tied together to the bedpost of brass, and Thick was snoring. He had somehow got her back into the white gown but had left the ties unfastened. It hardly covered her and despite the pain she could feel the gauzy touch of the old hat against one bare leg. Despite the darkness of the night she could faintly see the shreds of the long tasseled gown which he had ripped with his knife, muttering, ". . . Try to get big Thick in trouble, eh, try to make Thick look a fool. . . ." and had strewed viciously about the room, across the floor. A torn piece of the bodice was hanging over the closet door. And the little steamer trunk—how desperately she had found it, rummaged through the clothes of the long-dead woman. Cursing her, he had locked the little steamer in the cellar. Locked all escape away, then beaten her. And she had gone unconscious for an hour, for several hours, but there was no sleep for her. A bed she could not know—upon it violence that seemed not meant for her—this hour in which she could not sleep, arms drawn back and flesh captured with Thick's rope, so tightly that her hands were cold: she knew now the hunger of the abducted, knew how the poor girls felt when they were seized.

Four A.M. and she was one of the abducted. She wanted to stand at the window, hear a voice through the wall, find a flower pressed between the pages of a book, eat from a plate she recognized. But there was only the darkness smelling so unfamiliar and the ropes that cut and burned. She knew there was enormous penalty for what they had done to her—but she could not conceive of that, did not require that: she only wanted a little comfort, a bit of charity; with the awfulness, the unknowable, removed. Once when a girl—and she had been a girl—they had sent her away somewhere, and now the soreness, the sleeplessness, the sensation of invisible bruises reminded her of the hearth with an uneasy fire on it and an old woman threading buttons, an endless number of buttons—blue and white and violet—on a string. She was a child anything could be done to—and now, now a docile captive. And when Monica, the little girl, awoke about this hour with her nightmares, Margaret took them to be her own bad dreams, as if in soothing the child she could soothe herself.

But it wasn't soothing she wanted, it was a task or other to do. She hadn't believed Thick's beating, really, though it put her out for an hour or more. Later, lying strapped to the bed, she told herself it was what she might have expected: it was something done to abducted girls, that's all. She thought she had read a piece about a beating. And yet when it came it surprised her. Though thinking now, listening, looking back through the dark, she realized—this despite the article she had read—it was something they couldn't even show in films.

Because his sweat smelled raw when he tied her. And because after that, after he had grunted making the knots and cursed carrying the trunk down, he had become silent and watched her for a while, his precious radio telling them the time and starting a symphony, and then he had told her he might have to tape her mouth and she hardly heard it, listening to the low music and still feeling the hurt in her wrists and to herself considering that never before had her hands been tied.

And he remarked: "You don't look half bad. Like that. . . ."

But he hadn't forgiven her, because it was then that he stepped nearly out of sight across the room and she, hurting in the armpits as well as wrists, decided to try just how much freedom she really had—with only her arms drawn back to the post—and flexed a knee, the other knee, moved one foot far on the mattress and rolled her hips as much as she could. Until something told her she was being watched by Thick.

Then he came at her with the truncheon in his hand—it made her think of a bean bag, an amusement for a child—and wearing only his undervest and the trousers with the top two buttons open. He was in his stockinged feet and cigarette smoke was still coming out of his nose. She could see the dial of the little dry-cell radio in his glasses.

"I've beat girls before," whispering, holding the truncheon in the dark, bracing himself with one fat hand against the wall, "and I don't leave bruises. When it's done you won't be able to tell, you see. Plenty of girls—maids, the nude down in Robin's Egg Blue, the tarts who run the stitching machines, a kid named Sally. Used to operate in Violet Lane, I did. Gaslight scenes is my attraction. And if I happened to be without my weapon," raising a little the whiteness, the rubber, "the next best thing is a newspaper rolled and soaking wet. But here, get the feel of it, Miss." He reached down for her and she felt the truncheon nudging against her thigh, gently, like a man's cane in a crowd.

"It ain't so bad," he whispered.

She was lying face up and hardly trembling, not offering to pull her leg away. The position she was tied in made her think of exercises she had heard were good for the figure. She smelled gun oil—the men who visited the room had guns—and a sour odor inside the mattress. Perhaps the little one called Sparrow had left it there. Or even Thick, now standing beside her in the dark, because Thick liked to sleep on it in the afternoons. She remembered how earlier he had slept and how, after she and the child returned to the table, Monica had found a jack, as she thought she might, and won the game. And now, hearing the music, the symphony that old men were listening to in clubs, now she no longer would be able to play with Monica. She cared for nothing that Thick could do, but she would miss the games. There was a shadow on the wall like a rocking chair; her fingers were going to sleep; she thought that a wet newspaper would be unbearable.

Then something happened to his face. To the mouth, really. The sour sweat was there and the mouth went white, so rigid and distended that for a moment he couldn't speak: yet all at once she knew, knew well enough the kinds of things he was saying—to himself, to her—and in the darkness and hearing the faint symphonic program, she was suddenly surprised that he could say such things.

His arm went up quivering, over his head with the

truncheon falling back, and came down hard and solid as a length of cold fat stripped from a pig, and the truncheon beat into her just above the knee; then into the flesh of her mid-thigh; then on her hips; and on the tops of her legs. And each blow quicker and harder than the last, until the strokes went wild and he was aiming randomly at abdomen and loins, the thin fat and the flesh that was deeper, each time letting the rubber lie where it landed then drawing the length of it across stomach or pit of stomach or hip before raising it to the air once more and swinging it down. It made a sound like a dead bird falling to empty field. Once he stopped to increase the volume of the radio, but returned to the bedside, shuffling, squinting down at her, his mouth a separate organ paralyzed in the lower part of his face, and paused deceptively and then made a rapid swing at her, a feint and then the loudest blow of all so swiftly that she could not gasp. When he finally stopped for good she was bleeding, but not from any wound she could see.

For how many minutes he had kept it up, she did not know. Nor how long ago it was when he started. Because when she first opened her eyes he was snoring and the radio had changed. Comics were talking and she could not understand a word of it. And because now she was like a convent girl accepting the mysteries—and still Thick snored—and no matter how much she accepted she knew it now: something they couldn't show in films. What a sight if they flashed this view of herself on the screen of the old Victoria Hall where she had seen a few pictures with Michael. What a view of shame. She had always dressed in more modest brown, bought the more modest cod, prayed for modesty, desired it. Now she was hurt—badly hurt, she expected. And she remembered a woman in the basement flat being run down by a bus and telling it: and she felt that way herself—still bleeding—felt the damage deep inside, aching in unanticipated places, paining within. There wasn't any Mrs. Stickley now, and that other woman—in the basement flat—had died.

She felt that she herself could die. In those early hours she had not thought to scream. But now she was prostrate in Little Dora's Roost and even Little Dora, who hated them playing cards, was gone. And without the presence of some other woman, any woman, she could die. Thick had been too rough with her, treated her too roughly, and some things didn't tolerate surviving, some parts of her couldn't stand a beating. She hadn't even her free hands with which to rub them.

So finally she sobbed several times in this hour before the dawn. The moon had failed, the last clothes off her back were torn to shreds, the ginger cake they had given her at noon sat half-eaten and bearing her teeth marks in a chipped saucer atop the wardrobe. The moonlight's wash reached the window and fell across the brass and Margaret on the bed: a body having shiny knees, white gown twisted to the waist, arms stretched horizontal to the end of the bed and crossed; gray mattress-ticking beneath the legs whose calves were swollen into curves, and the head itself turned flat in the same direction she had raised one hip, away from the farther wall against which Thick snored; and a wetness under the eye exposed to the wash of light and the sobs just bubbling on the lips. Margaret inert, immobile, young woman with insides ruptured and fingers curling at the moment of giving sound to her grievance.

The sobs were not sweet. They were short, moist, lower than contralto, louder than she intended; the moanings of a creature no one could love. But Monica must have heard them—Monica whom Little Dora had brought back to the Roost after Thick himself had gone to sleep—or perhaps those sobs merely coincided with sobs of the child's own. Because when Margaret sobbed aloud, Monica sat up screaming.

The girl was given to having nightmares. All day long she was clever, turning away her inoculated arm, hiding inside her fists the little sharp black lines of her fingernails, walking on heels to prevent the sole of her left sandal from flapping, winning every afternoon at cards, though she had no use for horses. At the sink in the closet she spent time daubing herself with drops of Paradise Shore from a vial—shaped like a slipper—which she carried in a small white purse with a handle. She was forever finding hairpins on the floor and putting them quickly to her head. And she drank tea with her legs crossed and her good arm—the one without the scab—thrown over the back of the chair. Tall for her age, thin, not yet able to read, wearing socks that didn't reach to her ankles and a cameo ring tied from finger to wrist with a length of green ribbon, readily speaking of the pets—all suicides she said—which she had kept in their Farthing Maude flat, she was pale and bony and still smelling of dolls she had cared for, a girl expecting no favors in her bright-green dress, though sufficient enough in the daylight.

"She's being too friendly with the prisoner," Thick said whenever he could.

But at night there were horrors. At night she sweated her innocence and, bolting up in her shift, declared she'd been swimming in the petrol tank of a lorry, or watching three rubber dolls smartly burning, or sitting inside a great rubber tire and rolling down a steep cobbled hill in the darkness. And Margaret remembered these dreams.

Now Margaret's sobs and Monica's screams commenced together and continued together, variants of a single sound, screaming and weeping mingled. Margaret was lying with puffy red eyes closed but fully conscious of the mingling sounds. Monica was sitting upright on the brass bed next to her, not in the shift but merely in panties this night, and half the childish head of hair was down, the pins kept falling—a small body untouched, unidentified, except by arm bandage and the panties, and her eyes were shining open. Yet she was asleep, and between the two stripped beds and on the opposite wall the washed-back glow of the moon was lighting the cheap print in its glassless frame, print of a young woman who—in moonlight herself and with long hair drawn frontward across her chest, with two large butterflies sleeping upon her shoulders—was in the act of stepping into the silver pond to drink. So Margaret felt the two sounds coming from herself, starting from the same oppressive breast, as if the other half of sadness was quite naturally fear. And Margaret then opened her eyes and her face was toward Monica's bed and her arms were spasmodically flexing a little against rope and unyielding wrists and brass.

"Ducky," she whispered then, no longer sobbing, "Ducky. . . ."

Monica's head was lifted and the neck was stretched. There was a white thread hanging from the opened lips and it blew gently in the vibrations of the scream. The tooth-marked cake was on the wardrobe behind her.

"Ducky . . . wake up now, Ducky."

She was not awake yet, but she began to move: the graceless motions of the undressed dreaming child, fumbling off the bed, crouching and bending over as if the dream lay in the white innocent oval of her belly, stooped but holding the tiny hands out trembling to sense the night, and neither falling nor gliding across the distance between the beds yet coming on with a kind of limbless instinct, all disarrayed as an adult woman walking in the night. Until suddenly the little girl collapsed, fell forward, and buried the scream between Margaret's cheek and the ticking. And by touch of the child's skin, she knew that her own cheek was wet.

"Wake up, wake up," she whispered, and still Thick snored and she could not hold the girl.

But Monica's hands were clinging. She smelled the odors of soap and Paradise Shore and there was a hand upon her own shoulder making the flesh feel large, and the other small wedge-shaped hand was thrust between the mattress and her breast. Her lips were against the child's eyes and she could taste them. Somewhere she was losing blood, but there was no longer any sobbing or screaming. Only the melting dream, the feel of a dangling hairpin and at the foot of the empty bed next her own the dark-blue shade of one of Monica's sandals.

"Ducky," whispering against the eyes, "feeling a little better? There's a girl."

In the silence, glancing away from the face, she felt the child's fingers and touch of the cameo ring starting again at the round of her own shoulder; then traveling lightly away to the elbow and reaching the wrists, stopping. And followed by the other hand until both the child's arms were outstretched and come to a point atop her own, so that despite the cold and numbness she felt the grip, while somewhere below her waist she seemed to be sinking, caving in wall by tissue wall.

"Poor Margaret," said the little girl, "I could cry, I could. . . ."

"See can you do anything with the knots," she whispered then.

Monica knelt on the ticking near Margaret's head—a thin bent back, silver between the ribs, bowed as if for an old woman's drunken hand—and tried to work the rope ends.

"I can't," leaving off, soothing her fingers against the coolness of the brass. "What are we going to do?"

"Perhaps you could put a coat round me," she whispered at last. "If only Michael knew. . . ."

So the child fetched Little Dora's coat and spread it over Margaret and brought a glass of water and Banks' wife drank—some of it spilled and wet the mattress—and Monica dressed herself in the discarded green dress and sandals and socks. And on her own bare bed again: "Larry'll make him turn you loose. I promise."

"Yes. Go to sleep now, Monica." She watched the child lying firmly in the moonlight, watched two small hands carry the cake up and into the shadow of the mouth, listened to the rigid and fragile sounds of chewing. Later she heard Monica brush away the crumbs, lie still again.

Outside on a branch above the garbage receptacle, an oven tit was stirring: not singing but moving testily amidst the disorder of leaf, straw sprig, remnant of gorse, fluttering now and then or scratching, making no attempt to disguise the mood, the pallidness, which later it would affect to conceal in liveliness and muted song. A warbler. But a sleepless bird and irritable. Through drowsiness and barge-heavy pain she noticed the sounds of it and did not smile; saw rather a panorama of chimneys, fine rain, officers of the law and low yards empty of children; farther off there was a heap of tile and a young woman in rubber shoes, an apron and wide white cap, and there were bloodstains on the ticking.

She heard the door, and when it closed again it shook the picture of the woman bending at the pond. He was swaying in the room and stately drunk. Without feigning sleep and in innocence Margaret watched him, wondering what had changed him now, and smelled the dark rum which had stained the teeth, the lips, the tongue. The light was more than a wash—it seemed to come off the wardrobe's empty saucer, shine from the print of the pond, rise up from the worn flooring beneath his feet. Or the light was coming off the man himself.

Finally she understood this much: he was not fully dressed. The coat, the tie, the chemise-soft shirt, the undervest, were gone. And she was staring at naked arms, at white face and soot-black hair, at something silver that stretched and reflected the moon's pale tone from below his bare neck to the belted line of his trousers. And she thought that softly, ever so softly, he was humming as he swayed there, some sort of regimental march perhaps.

He moved then. Bringing the light, the glow, still closer—without any motion—he started down between the two brass beds, stopped—breathing near her shoulder—and fumbled in his pocket until he found and opened a little penknife that was only a sparkle before the curved sheet of steel. Despite the cold light of his chest she knew beforehand that his fingers would be hot, and his fingers were hot when, back turned to Monica, he stooped and reached—her own eyes were to the side and up and she saw the shining links like fish scales, and pressed to them the triangular black shape of the pistol—and began to cut. Once she saw his face, and it was the angel's whiteness except for a broken place at the corner of his mouth which set her trembling.

She waited and felt triumph while he cut. Then burning. For all his gestures were considerate, performed calmly and with care. There was sureness and the heated fingers. Yet there came his sound of breathing, and with exactitude he was yet slashing and the blade that went through Thick's ropes went into her wrists, her own wrists as well. They too began to bleed.

Even now, after how many hours, being able to move her arms, drag them back to her sides then cross them upon her stomach, chafe them, touch the welted wrists, even now there was little pleasure in it, feeling the scratches, cuts, stinging of the blood. "You've wounded me," she whispered, eyes to the ceiling and in darkness. "You cut me."

He said only: "I meant to cut you, Miss. . . ."

So sometime after 4 A.M. she tried to use her numb and sleeping arms, twice struck out at him, then found her hands, the bleeding wrists, the elbows, and at last her cheek going down beneath and against the solid sheen of his bullet-proof vest. At that moment sunlight roused the day's first warbling of the heavy oven tit, and Monica slipped away through the unguarded door.

Sparrow, having changed from wine to whisky and being drunk but not stately drunk, knelt in the middle of Larry's room and, surrounded by weapons of countless shape and caliber—black and oily, loaded, strewn across the floor and piled on the bed and on the horsehair rocker and the footstool, a collection of Webleys, Bren guns, automatics and revolvers to make the Violet Lane men whistle—and fumbling with string and paper, beret pushed all the way back and cupping the bald spot that protruded from the rear of his skull, fumbling and paying no attention to the woman crouched in the corner and sneering, tried to wrap something into a passable packet and failed until he cried, "Come over here, Little Dora, and give us a hand with this present for my boy Arthur."

7

SIDNEY SLYTER SAYS

Racing World Awaits Running of the Golden Bowl . . .

Classic Event Equivalent of Olympic Games . . .

Rock Castle's Owner: Pawn of Brutal Gang?

Somebody—angel of Heaven or Hell, surely—knew it all before. Somebody, possessed of prescience and having time stuck safely like a revolver in his pocket, knew all this already and went about the business as sure of satisfaction as a fellow robbing graves in a plague. Knowing Rock Castle's past, which was recorded; having only to know of that Danish blood which circulated beneath the skin, only to know that the fact of this Rock Castle—torn from his mare—predetermined the stallion's cyclic emergence again and again, snorting, victorious, onto the salt-white racing course of the Aegean shore; needing only this intelligence, that the horse existed and that the horse would win. Then to make off with him, one night to take him from the purple fields of the woman and groom too old, too feeble, and too wise to care; then to choose and pose one ignorant and hungry man as owner and with threats and violence and the pleasures of life to hold him until the race was won. Simple. Easy. Like taking sweets. . . . It might have been Sidney Slyter, mightn't it? Or Harry Bailey of East End? It might have been any one of us. . . . But it was Mr. Michael Banks. Because Mrs. Laval's been holding out her hand and drawing near, enfolding him. Because she told me so and has warned me off again, warned me off. But what do women know of such mysteries? They know too bloody much, I'd say. And Mrs. Laval, like all the rest of them—the gang of them—Mrs. Laval knew it all already. Every bit of it planned and determined in advance—the kiss, the dance, the jealous deaths—all of them beforehand set in motion like figures walking in the folds of the dirty shroud. . . . What now of Sidney Slyter's view of the world? What now of my prognostications? What of Marlowe's Pippet? And the sport? But what power, force, justice, slender hand or sacrifice can stop Rock Castle, halt Rock Castle's progress now? Sidney Slyter doesn't know. . . . Nonetheless, Sidney Slyter will report the running of the Golden Bowl for you. . . .

"Don't you know what eggs are good for, Michael?"

The hall bulb shone orange through the cracks round the door and moonlight was coming through the cobwebbed window. Across the floor boards the moon was one square and silver-tinted patch of light within which, in a silken heap, lay a stocking that wanted fingering; next to it a safety pin which, by moonlight and with point unclasped, looked charmed and filigreed, as personal as a young girl's fallen brooch. There was no sign of Cowles. There was nothing left of the jockey, not a boot or rubber jersey. Though out of the sounds of bottles smashing downstairs there came bursts of Jimmy Needles' laughter, loud and ribald and grievous.

It was 2 A.M. of the last night he spent alive—last darkness before the day and running of the Golden—and the covers were tossing. She had given a single promise and three times already made it good, so now he knew her habits, knew what to expect, the commotion she could cause in bed. And it was a way she had of rising and kicking off the covers with cartwheel liveliness and speed each time she lost a pearl—and she had lost three pearls—and asking him to hunt for it through the twisting and knotting of the sheets. Now the covers were cartwheeling and falling about his shoulders all at once and there was the fourth to find. At the end of the bedstead opposite the pillows she came to rest suddenly cross-legged and laughing, breathing so that he could see how far down she took the air.

"Don't ask me, Mike," hands above her head, hips wriggling a little at the apex of crossed legs, "I don't intend to help you. . . ." Then with a catch of sheet she idly daubed herself and laughed some more.

He came up crawling on hands and knees, still lagging after the tremor, the fanciful sex, and began to feel about in the tumult she had made of the sheets, himself not yet recovered from the breath of her own revival, the swiftness with which she turned from deep climactic love to play. As if she always saved one drop unquenched, the drop inside her body or on the tongue that turned her not back to passionate love but away from that and into attitudes of frolic. No moment of idleness or a yawn or slow recovery but each time surprising him by play and acrobatics, her fresh poses making his own dead self fire as if he had never touched her and making her body look tight and childish as if she had never been possessed by him.

"I can't find the bloody thing," he said.

"Go on," she said, and changed again, took one knee beneath her chin, "you find it." Then, while he searched beneath her pillow, felt down the center of the mattress and into the still warm hollows: "I've seduced you, haven't I, Mike," she said.

"You have," he answered. "Good as your word."

With Sybilline watching, he moved back and forth on the undulations of the springs, with moonlight striking across his spine, and his hands and knees softly sinking; and felt at last the opalescence, the hard tiny tear of pearl on its needle shank, and held it up by the point for her to see.

"You're a charmer, Mike," she said.

He reached out then to the skirt flung over the chair and stuck the pearl in the row of three. There were no pearls left in her reddish pompadour, only the thick round of the hair and, as if it had been rumpled, a coil coming down her neck and tickling. The bottles were still crashing below them and someone was playing the widow's piano so quickly, heavily, that Needles might have been running up and down the keyboard in his naked feet. But it was all bubbles of talk and musk and closeness in the room and Banks cared nothing for the noise. As he turned to face his Sybilline, began on hands and knees the several awkward motions it took to reach her, he knew remorse for the empty face of himself once more: because her eyes were big and brown, steady and temperate as those of a girl peering over a stile, while the rest of her was still animated, quivering, with the fun. Thrice she had taken him and he had thrice returned, riding into the bower that remains secretive and replete after blouse and skirt and safety pin, silks and straps, have all been discarded, flung about helter-skelter on the thorns. No more now, he was fast returning to the old man. While she, his Sybilline, was still tasting of that little shocking drop of incompletion that gave her a maiden's blush, a shine between the breasts, as if she was always ready for another go at it, another lovely toss.

After searching for all her pearls he was tangled in the covers now himself. His skin was gray. His head was hanging but he smelled the delicate stuff and blindly put his hand on her leg's underside, touched the mild flesh for an instant, then let his fingers drag away. She wriggled and was laughing.

"Be a sweet boy, Mike," she said, secluded with him from the party, moving her bare shoulders in childish sailor fashion, "and fetch the stocking."

So at two o'clock in the morning he labored off the bed—she gave his arm a push—and took several steps until the moonlight caught him round the skinny ankles. Standing there, with sheep passing outside through darkened fields and the jockey screaming the first bars of an enticing song, he could hear the girl behind him—and that was the fine thing about Sybilline, the way she could kiss and play and let her spangles fall, keep track of all the chemistry and her good time, and yet be sighing, sighing like a young girl in love.

He stooped, picked up the stocking, turned to hear her whistling through puckered lips.

Then: "I'll take that if you please, sweet Michael." She held the length of silk in her hands and he was scrambling over the tossed pillows, down the crumpled sheets, until the two of them were facing and once more cross-legged. The pharmacist's cure for women was on the edge of the sink, the smells were of the shores of paradise. Before his eyes and with the ends of her fingers, Sybilline drew the stocking out full length, held it swinging by the wide top and little toe, then in a quick gesture ran the whole porous line of it across her face and under her nose, just touching her nose, smelled it deeply and winked as she did so. And suddenly made a flimsy ball of it and with one hand lightly on his knee, reached forward and thrust the round of silk between his widespread legs and against the depths of his loin, rubbing, pushing, laughing. He flushed.

"You see," whispering, "you can win if you want to, Mike, my dear. But that's all for now." With lively arm she threw the balled stocking at the dusty moonlit glass and hopped off the bed.

He watched her dance round to the chair, dangle the blouse and skirt, replace the pearls and do a faint jazz step that kept her moving nowhere. Then she posed in the unbuttoned blouse and her fingers were sending off kisses and her legs, friendly and white and long, were the legs he had seen bare in the undergarment ads. Then she whispered through the oval of the skirt she was just dropping over her head: "Put on your trousers, Mike . . . we'll join the fun downstairs."

They stepped into the light of the orange bulb, held hands, walked along the widow's carpet to the start of the rail with grapes carved on the post. The hallway smelled of dust and nuptials; a rag was lying on the carpet. "We'll go down together," she said, and gave his arm a pinch. "We'll let them see we're untidy. But Michael," holding him midway on the stairs, "all the girls will love you, Michael. You're alluring! So don't forget, Mike, come back for me." And she kissed him, she whom he would never kiss in privacy again.

"I couldn't lose you, Syb."

She laughed for the two of them at the bottom of the stairs and her hair was redder than at any time that day. The lamplight shone upon it—lamps were lit all about the room, small bulbs and large, glass shades chiming and tinkling and strung with beads—and her eyes were brown and moist.

"There's that lovely girl!" shouted the widow, "and our funny boy. And look what she's done to him!"

Not only Jimmy Needles was playing the piano, but Larry as well, jockey and Larry having a duet together side by side and beating on the keys with nearly equal strength. On the bench before the upright, the little man in color and the large man in navy blue—hour by hour the wrinkles in the dampened suit were flattening—kept talking all the while they played and a bottle of rum stood on the seat between them. And Little Dora tried to listen. Sunk in a velvet armchair, wearing her lopsided matron's hat with a bit of feather now, her upper lip of pale hair wet with gin, eyes surly and black behind the glasses, stretched and recumbent on cushions as near as possible to the piano bench, she watched them, listened, in a torporous and deadly mood.

Sparrow was there. He was drinking whisky out of the widow's cup. The widow's daughter was in the crowd—a big girl in a child's dress pulled high who sat straight up and kept both hands on her knees, laughing and smiling out of a loose mouth and enormous eyes. And all the room was brown and filled with smoke and toy alligators and donkeys. Newspapers were strewn across the rug faded and worn with the footpaths of long-dead residents. A portrait of a Spanish nobleman hung above the mantel on which there burned a candelabra with smoky wicks and molten wax; and duplicates of Little Dora's chair, soft mauve contrivances on wheels, made humps along the walls. In volume nearly as loud as the piano the black wireless was turned up and an orchestra played out of the tufted speaker.

Kissing, noise, and singing: a late hour in the widow's parlor, and Banks saw Sparrow wave, watched Sybilline sit on the arm of Little Dora's chair and swing her foot, and noticed that the widow was keeping her eye on him. Plump, wearing the tasseled shawl, she suddenly leaned over Syb and the slouching woman, and after a moment

Dora jerked round her head and stared at him. Then all three were laughing—even his own dear girl—and he started toward them, took a place at the jockey's side.

A barracks song was coming from the coffin box of the piano, old, fast-stepping. A golden mermaid stood holding a pitchfork on the ebony and she was bounded by wreaths, her fishtail curved over her head. Scars and finger-length burns marked the ebony, ivory was missing from the keys. Banks leaned against the trembling wood, and there was a pile of tattered sheet music ready to fall from the top and he had never heard such noise. Yet Larry went on talking—audibly enough, considering—and the jockey was nodding and beating upon the last key of the scale.

". . . And I told the Inspector he was making a horrible botch of it. I said it would never do. Who's pulling the strings I told him and he got huffy, huffy, mind you. I said the killing of the kids was no concern of mine but the hanging of Knifeblade was not acceptable, not in the least acceptable. You'd best not interfere, I said. There's power in this world you never dreamed of, I told him. Why, you don't stand a showing even with a little crowd at the seaside . . . and you'd better not bother with my business or my amusements. . . ."

"But didn't he try to stick you none the same," said the jockey.

"He did, but he failed. I knew him in Artillery, I knew his line. . . ."

Banks listened, looked at the white craven half of his face, the slicked black hair, the fingers hammering. He saw the man lift the bottle several times to his lips.

The jockey's sleeves were puffing out, the small black boots were hanging limp, one hand snatched down the goggles and through isinglass he peered at the single key and at the two gray fingers he was striking it with—a rider who had a face shot full of holes and shoulders like the fragile forks of a wishbone on either side of the hump inside the silk. Banks put a sheet of the music on the rack and said, "Play us this piece, Needles. . . ." But the jockey did not reply.

There was a fire in the kitchen and it was Sybilline who told him to take the chair—"Don't you know what eggs are good for, Michael?"—and stood near him with her smile and the flush creeping up her cheek. They formed a regular crew: his Syb, the widow, the other one who looked as if she wanted to fight. Syb's throat was bare, the widow had plump hips and she was giggling. He could smell them: above the heat and moisture of the fire, the spice and flour odors of the laden shelves, the sweetness of old tarts and bread, he could smell the women strongest. And Sybilline kissed him immediately—leaning over, putting her face into his and her hand upon his neck—so that the other two could see. Still with mouths together, he found her breast for a moment and opened his eyes, saw the widow smiling—but it was a smile set and strained as if she could hardly keep from offering advice—and the other woman was smiling and Banks didn't care.

"Get out of here, Sparrow," the widow said all at once

and looked down at him, became dimpled and rosy-cheeked again. Then Syb left him, stepped away with her compassionate mouth dissolving, becoming part of a pretty face again, and he could think of nothing except the stocking she had left upstairs—though they were roughing it in the parlor next to the kitchen and flinging about, dancing with the widow's girl, intent, all of them, on a smashing.

"Now, Mike, you'll have to eat," she murmured, and put a hand to her escaping loop of hair.

"But you been cheating, Sybilline," the widow said then, "you been going out of turn. The lady of the house has first prerogative and you been spoiling the order, Sybilline—if you please—you ain't been allowing me my prerogative." The little woman, youthfully plump except in the legs—she was standing on wiry, well-shaped legs—was preoccupied: it may have been she alone he smelled.

"Syb's always been a cat," said Little Dora, "first at the fellows, first in bed. She's a sister of mine but she's irresponsible, she is." And Banks could tell that this one, a fighter with her violet shadows and loosened boots, was interested: but probably she'd want to kill him first. There were no smiles behind those thick corrective spectacles.

"Well, Syb can do the cooking then," said the widow, and sat down beside him.

"I'll cook, I'd do anything for Michael!" There was the light step, the grace, the cheer, as she tossed her head and reached for the pan and the bowl of pure-white oval eggs. She got the butter on her fingertips and licked them, her blouse was untucked again and he could see the skin; the eggs were pearls and she was cracking the white shells with her painted nails. The widow was lighting a cigarette. Though he was watching Syb, he found that he was stroking the little widow's cheek and coming to like her in the kitchen with no one, except these three, to notice.

Beyond the half-opened door the parlor crowd sang "Roll Me Over in the Clover" and the name of Jimmy Needles was screamed out several times. But the women round him seemed not to hear; he hardly heard himself; the women were ganging up on him, doing a job on him. All three were noticing and he tried to pay no attention. They watched him eat. All three were smiling and taking his measure and he didn't mind. It was Sybilline who made him use the sauce.

"Here," reaching, tilting the thin brown bottle, "meat sauce is fine on fried eggs, Michael . . . didn't you know?"

The smell of the women—girlish, matronly—and the smell of the meat sauce were the same. As soon as it spread across his plate it went to his nostrils and they might not have bothered with their clothes, with procrastination. He kept his face in the plate and kept lifting the fork that had one prong bent, a prong that stuck his tongue with every mouthful. Brown and broken yellow, thick and ovarian, his mouth was running with the eggs and sauce while the whisky glasses of the women were leaving rings.

"Fetch him a slice of bread, Sybilline, he don't want to leave none of it on the china. . . ."

He shut his eyes and did not know whose hand it was, but the hand closed in a grip that made him slide forward on the chair and groan.

"You girls wait for me," said the widow in a voice he could hardly hear. Then: "You're a charmer, Mike!" and Sybilline was blowing him a kiss.

With his hands in his pockets, shirt collar open about the windpipe and the two muscles translucent at the back of his skinny neck, frowning and keeping his head down, he followed the swinging shawl into the din, the smoke, the noise of the piano that seemed to be playing on the strength of a grinding motor inside the box, though Larry and the jockey were still side by side on its bench. The widow stopped to fix her daughter's skirts and he bumped against the softest buttocks he had ever known, and apologized.

"I could love you right here," she whispered, "I really could. . . ."

He knew that. It was not the place for him exactly, but there was the sauce all over his lip and he thought that in another moment almost anywhere might do.

They reached the stairs in time. The corner turned, the hat tree with its multiple short arms thrust out in shadow, the carpeting, the widow's rail, the dust and orange bulb —suddenly the bedchambers were near and he was climbing. Up how many times, how many times back down. And it was merely a matter of getting up those stairs, and taking the precautions, and tumbling in, shagging with the widow as the night demanded. He saw her at the top for a moment; stumbled and paused and, clutching the rail, stared, while beneath the bulb she stood squeezing the tiny plump hands together.

Then she took hold of him, and behind the door at the end of the hall he dropped his trousers in the widow's sleeping chamber, heard her quick footsteps round the bed and in his hands caught the plumpness of the hips. Then under the wool those softest buttocks he had ever known. And he snapped off a stay of whalebone, flung it aside as he might a branch in a tangled wood; to his mouth drew her down and rubbed the sauce against her. She giggled and there was a dilating in the stomach.

"Go gently, Mr. Banks," fending, giggling, "go sweetly, please."

There was no cartwheeling now, no silk-stocking coil, no blushing or line of verse. Only the widow on the comforter and in his mouth the taste of eggs which had done the job for him. The moon had passed by the widow's room, but a transom was opened to the orange dimness of the hall. And under her three small rocking chairs with cushions, upon her bed—it was narrow and deep—and her rack of short broad night dresses and her stumpy bedside lamp, upon everything she owned or used there fell the rusty and sedentary light that, guiding no one, still burns late in the corridors of so many cheap hotels. The drawers were all half-open in her wardrobe; a pair of silver shears and a babyish fresh pile of curls lay on a table top before which she last had been trimming her dead ends of curls.

How long were the nights of love, how various the lovers. Holding his throat, standing in bare feet and with one hand wiping the hair back from his eyes, he stared down at the widow's cheeks again. It was her cheeks he had been attracted to and once more beside the bed he saw the tiny china-painted face with the eyelids closed, the ringlets damp across the top, the small greasy round cheeks he had wanted to cup in both his hands.

"Don't leave," whispering, not opening her eyes, "don't leave me yet, Mr. Banks."

In the hall he put on his trousers and shirt and took the stairs with caution. He was fierce now, dry but fierce. If there were prospects ahead of him he would take them up. There were shadows, tracks worn through the carpet by naked feet. More shadows, a depth of shadows, and not a vow to make or sentiment to express now on these old stairs—only the steepness and the wallside to guide his shoulder. Below, in the center of a love seat's cushion, he could see the outline of a hat and pair of clean white gloves.

"Mister . . ." He stopped, leaned his head against dusty wall plaster, and saw the big girl's figure at the start of the bannister below, made out her eyes and heard the moist and childish voice. She wore a sweater round her shoulders now. "Mister," the voice came fearfully, "there's someone wants to see you. A lady, Mister."

"I should imagine so!" He waited, then descended without noise, except for the brushing of his clothes against the wall, until he was only a step or two above the widow's girl. "I suppose you're not referring to yourself." He watched the loose lips, the eyes that brightened, watched the closing and opening of the sweater.

"She's a lady, Mister. She's at the other door. She give me half a crown to find you, and she told me not to get the whole house up, she did."

He nodded, leaned forward, gently kissed the girl.

She did not try to move, as if he had ordered her to remain exactly there by the darkened post with grapes. He paused at the love seat and noticed the red beret beside the hat and pair of gloves. The corridor smelled of water in the bottoms of purple vases and the piano was banging just beyond this emptiness. He kicked something—a cat's dish perhaps—and it slid down the passageway ahead of him. Then the wall was warm to his touch and he knew that behind it was the width of the kitchen chimney, briefly and in darkness saw the meat-sauce bottle and Syb's painted nails.

He heard an engine running. He stepped into the pantry, one of several pantries, bare now without hanging goose or cutlery or stores of brandy, and faced the misty dew-drenched opening of the door. There was light coming in the windows—brass rods cut them, but they were curtainless—and he stood so that he was lighted by one of the windows just as she was visible against the sheet of fog. With a coat swinging, hair down to her shoulders, she was leaning in the doorway and her thin legs were crossed. When she heard him she turned her face, white at this hour, and dropped her burning cigarette—not outside, but into the shadows on the floor.

"Annie . . . good God, is it you?"

She laughed only. One long shank of the golden hair dragged across in front of her and buried the little wet coat lapel. The face then, the cheek, seemed set in gold. Arm hanging, body still tipped and ankles crossed, she made no movement other than a small twisting as if she were trying to scratch against the jamb.

"But you, Annie, I hadn't expected you!"

"Well," taking the hair in her fingers, holding it across her mouth, speaking through hair, "I shan't be bad or deceitful to an old friend. But I can tell a thing or two." And abruptly, as he smelled the dampness on her shoulders and reached for her, "You're sexed up, aren't you? The chap next door's been kissing and the girl next door has found him out!" She was twenty years old and timeless despite the motor car waiting off under the trees. At three o'clock in the morning she was a girl he had seen through windows in several dreams unremembered, unconfessed, the age of twenty that never passes but lingers in the silvering of the trees and rising fogs. Younger than Syb, fingers bereft of rings, she would come carelessly to any door, to any fellow's door.

"You'll have to lift me up," she cried, "I've got this far but I can't take another step." Then laughed when he raised her, gold hanging down and legs swinging at the knees, cheekbones making little slashes beneath the skin, eyes big and black and body that had been tipping, leaning, all collected now, wrapped in the coat and carried high against his chest. They sat on the bare pantry floor in a corner and through the adjacent windows came the misty streams like two searchlight shafts touching and crossing just beyond their feet.

"Bottle's in the pocket. Have a drink if you want to." He did, though first he put his palms on either side of the chilly jaw and leaned down to Annie's mouth. With the hair spread out, eyes closed, her head was pressed between his kiss and the hard empty floor. And the searchlights moved steadily, the engine idled—it was smooth, low, indifferent—in the blackness of the roadside and dripping chestnut tree.

"I'm sexed up, too," she said from the crook of his arm, and he uncapped the bottle with his teeth. The crashing octaves, Needles singing solo, the screams and sounds of boots hardly reached them here, though Annie remarked about the party and, after thinking, said she did not want to go to it.

He opened her coat directly and ran his hand inside, up lisle and tenderness until he found the seam, the tight rolled edge and drops of warmth against his fingertips, and said, ". . . You want me to, you really want me to?" She stood up then—he hadn't known that she could stand—and with fingers steadying on his shoulders lifted first one tiny knife-heeled slipper and the other, bending each leg sharply at the knee, swinging alternate thin calves in an upward and silent dancing step, removed the undergarment and the slippers, and came down slowly, slowly, across his lap.

"I want you to."

Later, when they were dying down and moments before she slept: "That Hencher," she said, "evict him, why don't you, Mike . . . throw the bastard out." And the jaws, the cheeks, the eyelids all grew colder and he left her there for the driver of the lacquered car.

Slowly, slowly, he went back up the hall with hands outstretched and thinking of all the girls. He saw the hat tree's shadow, passed the love seat and the staircase, empty now, and thought, she's gone off looking at her half a crown. Good thing.

He took a breath then and blinking through the smoke, rubbing his lips and blinking, holding Annie's gin bottle halfway to his lips and then forgetting it, found Larry towering in the parlor and Little Dora shouting up at him. Dora was wearing the jockey's striped racing cap and the long flat tongue of the visor protruded sideways from her trembling head.

"Take it off," she shouted, "let's see what you got!"

Sparrow, Jimmy Needles and the rest were crowded round them, laughing and showing their teeth through smoke and the white light of lamps with the shades ripped off now. But Larry towered, even while Dora caught him by the shirt, and there was the perfect nose, the black hair plastered into place, the brass knuckles shining on the enormous hand, and the eyes, the eyes devoid of irises. Tomorrow he would wear green glasses. For now he was drunk, drunk into a stupor of civility and strength, that state of brutal calm, and only a little trickle of sweat behind the ear betrayed his drunkenness.

"Come on, come on, you full-of-grace," pushing up against him, tearing the shirt, "let's see what you got!"

The pearl buttons came off the shirt and Banks stepped no closer, though Sybilline was there and laughing on one of Larry's arms. "Oh, do what Little Dora says," he heard her cry, "I want you to!" And there was a bruise, a fresh nasty bruise, beneath Syb's eye.

It was not a smile nor look of tolerance, but some wing-tip shadow—he was cock of this house—that passed across his face and Banks thought Larry had swayed. Yet he removed the wrinkled coat, allowed Sybilline to pull the holster strings, ungird him, allowed Little Dora to flap against him and rip off the shirt and, after Sparrow had undone the ties, once more waited while Dora took the undervest away in her claws. They cheered, slapping the oxen arms, slapping the flesh, and cheered when the metal vest was returned to him—steel and skin—and the holster was settled again but in an armpit naked now and smelling of scented freshener.

Larry turned slowly round so they could see, and there was the gun's blue butt, the dazzling links of steel, the hairless and swarthy torso of the man himself. In the process of revolving he looked at Sparrow, who went out then to the hired vehicle parked before the boarding house.

"For twenty years," shouted Dora again through smoke opaque as ice, "for twenty years I've admired that! Does anybody blame me?" Banks listened and amidst breaking glass, the tumbling of the mauve-colored chairs, for a moment met the eyes of Sybilline, his Syb, eyes in a lovely face pressed hard against the smoothest portion of Larry's arm which—her face with auburn hair was just below his shoulder—could take the punches. Banks looked away.

He left the gin bottle on a bolster and sprawled out shivering on the love seat. They were finished with the final stanza of poor Needles' song. He could very nearly taste the dawn, the face peering up out of a basin, becoming old again, his full and wasting twenty-five. But he listened, reached forward through the dark and then the shadow was in front of him, Dora's bit of beard and a glimpse of the fibrous and speckled hams, and he would have laughed except for the last jump inside of him.

"Got a cigarette," he asked her softly, and started trembling.

He was alone, finally, all alone and sore and the cartwheeling sheets were piled in a white heap on the planking off the foot of the bed. The last of them was gone; love's moonlight was no longer coming through the glass; but there was light, the first gray negative light of dawn. The mate of the oven tit had found a branch outside his window and he heard its damp scratching and its talk. Even two oven tits may be snared and separated in such a dawn. He listened, turned his head under the shadows, and reflected that the little bird was fagged. And he could feel the wet light rising round all the broken doors, the slatted crevices, rising round the fens, the dripping petrol pump, up the calves and thighs of the public and deserted visions of the naked man—the fire put out in the steam-bath alley, the kitchen fire drowned, himself fagged and tasteless as the bird on the sick bough. But a sound reached him and for a while he followed it: "Cowles . . . Mr. Cowles? Mr. Cowles?" The widow's voice faded down in the direction of the barren pantry and open door.

He let it go. He smelled the pillow touched by too many heads, smelled the dry sweat of a night no more demanding—gone the pale rectangle from which he had plucked the stocking, gone all the fun of it. He thought of water against his lips but he could not move, stretched upon his back and caught. But he must have moved his leg because suddenly he felt it pricked, a sharp little pain in the skin, some bit of foreign matter. He reached down slowly and took it in two fingers, raised it high before his face: a single pearl on a pin that had been bent, but a lovely rose color in the center where it held the light. Idly he began to turn the pearl between his fingers. The hand hovered, fell, and he lost the pearl for good.

The shot went off just below his window. It was a noise in the very room with him, like a hand clapped upon his ear, and he thought of Jimmy Needles, the shoulder holster on the silver breast, thought of Sybilline and the widow. Then he was out of the bed, across the room and running.

He reached the street before the gunshot sound had died, ran into the dawn bareheaded and in time to see the warbler flying straight up from the thick brown tree with its song turned into a high and piping whistle. There were the frozen headlamps and black dripping tires of a double-decker parked across the street; a cottage with a hound clamoring inside; a poster showing bunched horses on a turn; an empty cart drawn back from the road. And at the corner of the boarding house, sprawled on the stones, the body of a child in a bright-green dress and, crouched over it, the puffing constable. A wet and sluggish sun was burning far-off beyond the wet foliage and crooked roofs.

He stopped—arms flung wide—then ran at the constable.

Because he recognized the child—she had always been coming over a bridge for him—and because now there was smoke still circling out of the belly, smoke and a little blood, and she lay with one knee raised, with palms turned up. And the old man crouching with drawn gun, touching the body to see where his shot had gone, old man with a star of burst veins in the hollow of either cheek, with his warts, the old lips that were ventricles in the enormous face, with brass and serge and a helmet like a pot on the head—there was nothing he could do but smash his fist against that puffing face. He did, and sent the helmet rolling.

The mists were drifting off, the leaves uncurling, the helmet was rattling about the street. And he kept driving the man, fighting the constable farther and farther away from the dead child, watching one of the mournful and unsuspecting eyes turn green and slowly close. Scuffling, panting himself, trying to take his punches with care, aiming at the blood that had started between the two front teeth. Then suddenly the constable—old, with a neck of cow's kidneys tied round by the high blue collar, and a nose that hooted in the struggle—gave it all back to him, blow for telling blow, finding his mark, punching in with the slobber and vehemence of his age. There was a straight look in his watering good eye, a quick and heavy hunching in the shoulders. His long hair, black and mixed with gray, went flying.

"Down you go, you little Cheapside gambler!"

The old man struck him full in the chest, once in the face, and once again on skin and cartilege of the aching chest. He fell, lay still—blindly reaching out for the little girl in green—and the constable drew back the boot furnished by the village constabulary and kicked him. After a moment of wheezing and blood-wiping, the old man strapped on the helmet, fixed his brass and replaced the warm revolver, took up his pipe from the mossy curb, and rubbing his arms and shins, disappeared to slowly climb the footbridge that was a hump of granite beneath the electric cables and ancient dripping trees.

It'll be a jolly evening, Mike, he dreamed, and the sun was shining on his lip when Jimmy Needles came out and dragged him to the safety of the house.

8

SIDNEY SLYTER SAYS

Freak Accident Halts Famous Race . . .

Thousands Witness Collision at End of Day . . .

Fatal Crash Brings Solemn Cry from Crowd . . .

. . . A beautiful afternoon, a lovely crowd, a taste of bitters and light returning to the faces of heroic stone—one day there will be amusements everywhere, good fun for our mortality. He has whistled; he has flicked his cigarette away; alone amidst women he has gone off to a fancy flutter at the races. And redeemed, he has been redeemed—for there is no pathetic fun or mournful frolic like our desire, the consummation of the sparrow's wings. . . .

In the paddock and only minutes before the running of the Golden Bowl on a fast track and brilliant afternoon —high above them now the sun was burst all out of shape—Michael Banks and Needles listened to the dying of the call to saddle. A plaster held Banks' lips together at a corner of the mouth and impaired his speech; the jockey was sallow but Banks wore a large rose with leaves in his lapel; Lovely the stableboy kept whispering: "What a gorgeous crowd! Coo, what a gorgeous crowd!" They had tied down Rock Castle's tongue and now the horse's mouth was filled with a green scum. Round the paddock the crowd was twenty deep and silent, save for a rat-faced man at the spectator's rail who several times cocked his eyebrows, pointed at the silver horse, and said: "Rock Castle? Go on, I wouldn't take your money. Poor old nag."

Farther down, a mare set up a drumming with her hind hoofs, then was calmed. Men attending in the paddock spoke soothing words; a black horse was being led in tight circles, again the chestnut mare was dancing.

Banks took the camel's hair coat off the jockey's back, bared the resplendent little figure to sun and crowd. "Well, Needles," carefully hanging the coat on his arm, "Cowles always said he'd run like fire. Well, up you go, Needles."

Before he could take the jockey's leg in his hands, he heard the sounds of light and girlish hurrying, saw her stoop beneath the rail, saw the hair and the swinging coat similar to Needles'.

"Oh, good," cried Annie, "you've not started off! I thought I'd bring you luck."

"You can't come in the paddock," glancing about for the detectives, "you haven't any business here!"

"Oh, but I have, I have."

And Annie reached toward the jockey then, and even while Banks gripped the blown-out silken sleeve, she caught hold of Jimmy Needles' face in both her hands, leaned down and kissed the tiny wrinkles of his lips. Drawing away, golden hair uncombed and a printed card dangling from her buttonhole, breeze carrying off her laugh: "Oh, haven't I always wanted to? Haven't I just wanted to?"

Somebody whistled in the crowd.

"Tell you what," straightening the green glasses, cutting his profile across the sun, "I'll make it up to you. I'll make it up for the twenty years. A bit of marriage, eh? And then a ship, trees with limes on the branches, niggers to pull us round the streets, the Americas—a proper cruise, plenty of time at the bar, no gunplay or nags. Perhaps a child or two, who knows?"

Arm in arm, Larry and Little Dora, one tall and tough, the other squat and tough, strode along until they approached one hired car in a line of cars and, opening the rear doors, stooping, lifted Margaret from under a shabby quilt and off the floor, and, each gripping an arm and wrapping round her body the coat that belonged to Dora, started back still talking—now across Margaret's hanging head—about the streets and niggers and limes of the Americas.

"Coo, what a gorgeous crowd!"

But even the crowd was fixed. There were no more islands of space between the stands and the white threads of the rails upon which the slovenly men were chalking, erasing, again chalking up their slates. Yet Thick had made a way for himself and could see all he needed to of the first turn; through long dark binoculars Sybilline watched the final turn; and in the center of the oval's roses, crouched down between two bushes, armed and grinning, Sparrow waited for signs of trouble, ready to shoot or turn as best he could to any threatened portion of the course. Sparrow always liked a race.

Banks saw nothing of the crowd but kept his eyes on Sybilline. Not once did she glance his way—though he was watched. He was being watched all right. Among the men on the rail he noticed the three who had accosted him, and wondered whether they would fling their bombs into a crowd just to bring one man down.

Then he heard the horses drifting slowly up from behind, the string of them unlimbering in the slow canter before the start. One of the jockeys was singing and Banks could not bear to raise his eyes, could not bear to see Rock Castle in that winding and nervous line, afraid to know that the horse had come this far. He kept his eyes down, began again his pushing and shoving, and there were only shoes to see: the open toes, pieces of nicked leather, buckles. Heel the color of a biscuit, slipper covered with diamond dust and glue, some child's boot tied with string. Shoes in motion or fixed at isolated angles amidst tickets, sweet wrappers, straws, and with the bit of stocking or colored sock or bare ankle protruding—shoes which end to end would have made a terrible marching column round the track the horses were soon to charge upon. He could not bear the faces, refused to look at them. On his own face the fresh plaster held the split corners of his mouth together and he was clean—it had not been easy to visit the Baths again but he had forced himself—and his narrow cheeks were shaved and his tie was straight. The only dirt was sleeplessness and he could not rid himself of that.

"Now, Sally, you'll see a little more from here," somebody said.

He kept pushing, trying to get beyond the crowd, trying for the north corner, where it was thinner at least. He saw the man with the gray tea-party topper and new supply of yellow, brown, green tickets stuck in the band, and he lowered his eyes again, thought of the night before and drinking-glasses with lipstick on the rims. He thought he should like to try it, try some of that, with Margaret. Once he stopped and lifted his head, but she was not in sight.

Then he was walking easily and into the glare of the hot sun, past the ranked petrol-smelling rows of empty cars, and there were little shattering bursts of light off the wipers and chrome and door handles, and only a few other people strolling here, laughing or pausing in the weeds by the rail. He leaned against a Daimler and tried to breathe. He noticed the pock-faced girl and it was clear she had found her quid: a big man with a sandy bush of mustache and gold links in his cuffs was holding her round the buttocks with one great hand. Another man and woman had their elbows side by side on the rail.

"Look," said the woman, and he heard no inflection, no rise or fall in her voice, "they're off."

Far away, back under clock and pennants, a terrible cheering went up. But it was the woman's clear statement that made him sick. He pulled his hand away from the radiator cap, set his foot down from the bumper, and tried to get close to her before the thirteen horses of the field should pass.

"Charlie, you're going to owe me a tonic," the woman said.

He heard the sound of hoofs and managed to stumble into the shadow of the pair by the rail. He nodded to the woman and she smiled, spoke again to her husband—"You might as well tear up your ticket!"—and he felt the coming breeze, watched a long hair on his sleeve. The mustached man had his back to the race. The girl was trying to see over his shoulder but he prevented her. And then the hair was saved between his fingers and he looked up, began to choke.

The blinders, the tongue tied down, the silver neck sawing in stride; the riders coming knee to knee with tangle of sticks and the noise; dust, the dangerous dust, rising high as a tall tree, and pebbles flying out like shots. He put an arm across his face, whispered *Margaret,*

Margaret, and in the vacuum, the sudden silence, heard no hoofs, no roar, but only the thwacking of the crops and the clear voice of Jimmy Needles: "Make way for the Prince of Denmark . . . out of my path, St. James. . . ." He knew he must put a stop to it.

"You can't do that! Grab him, for God's sake, Charlie!"

But he was over the rail then and into the dust at last. It was a long way to go—directly across the track in the open sun—and he stumbled, tried to hold the hat. He heard his heart—far away a child seemed to be beating it down the center of a street in the End—heard the sound of air being sucked beneath the spot where the constable had landed two heavy blows, and his feet were falling upon the same loose earth so recently struck by iron.

He hadn't the strength to climb the second fence, instead went between the bars, going down, seeing his own dead shoe for a moment, feeling his hand slipping off the whitewash. Then he was on the green, splashed through an artificial pond, ran headlong into roses and hedges that came up to his shins. It was a park, a lovely picture of a park with a mad crowd down one edge and thirteen horses whirling round. His shoe came down on the blade of a shears some gardener had overlooked. He nearly fell. He would have to be fast, very fast, to stop them now.

He heard his shoes snapping off the thorns and trampling the grass, and yet he seemed only to be drifting, floating across the green. But it was a good run, an uphill run. The wind was catching his saliva when suddenly he veered round the man rising up between the rose bushes with a pistol. He saw the gun-hand, the silencer on the barrel like a medicine bottle, the quickness of Sparrow's waist-high aim, and then felt both shots approaching, overtaking him, going wild. And he reached the third and final fence, crawled through.

The green, the suspended time was gone. The child pounded on his heart with anonymous rhythm and he found that after all he had been fast enough. There were several seconds in which to take the center of the track, to position himself according to the white rails on his right and left, to find the approaching ball of dust ahead and start slowly ahead to encounter it. Someone fired at him from behind a tree and he began to trot, shoes landing softly, irregularly on the dirt. The tower above the stands was a little Swiss hut in the sky; a fence post was painted black; he heard a siren and saw a dove bursting with air on a bough. I could lean against the post, he thought, I might just take a breath. But the horses came round the turn then and once more his stumbling trot was giving way to a run. And he had the view that a photographer might have except that there was no camera, no truck's tailgate to stand upon. Only the virgin man-made stretch of track and at one end the horses bunching in fateful heat and at the other end himself—small, yet beyond elimination, whose single presence purported a toppling of the day, a violation of that scene at Aldington, wreckage to horses and little crouching men.

The crowd began to scream.

He was running in final stride, the greatest spread of legs, redness coming across the eyes, the pace so fast that it ceases to be motion, but at its peak becomes the long downhill deathless gliding of a dream until the arms are out, the head thrown back, and the runner is falling as he was falling and waving his arm at Rock Castle's on-rushing silver shape, at Rock Castle who was about to run him down and fall.

". . . the blighter! Look at the little blighter go!"

Quietly, holding the girl's arm in the midst of the crowd: "Let me have the binoculars, Sybilline." Larry removed his green glasses, blinked once, and, still holding her arm so that the brass knuckles were brilliant and sunken into her flesh, looked through binoculars until the cloud went up.

"He's crossed us," whispered Sybilline, "he's crossed us, hasn't he?"

Out beyond the oval and past the broken threads of the rail the cloud stopped short and rose, spending itself dark as an explosion's smoke. Then Larry was done and Sybilline took a look for herself: dust abruptly curling, settling down, horses lying flat with reins in the air, small riders limping among the animals or in circles or off toward the fence. And the silver horse was on its side with Banks and Jimmy Needles underneath. And three dirty-white Humber ambulances were racing up the track.

"Take me out to him . . . take me out to him, please."

But in the confusion—they passed the lined white faces

of the man with tickets, the woman's husband Charlie, the older woman with chocolates smeared on her hands again—Larry and Syb and Little Dora hustled her behind the stands and out to the enormous car waiting in the line of cars, bundled her under the rags and quilting on the car floor. Thick was already sweating behind the wheel.

9

It was a heavy rain, the sort of rain that falls in prison yards and beats a little firewood smoke back down garret chimneys, that leaks across floors, into forgotten prams, into the slaughterhouse and pots on the stove. It fell now on the roof of the stables in the Highland Green area and caused the trough beneath the pump to overflow, tore cobwebs off small panes of glass, filled wood and stone with the sound of forced rainwater. Timbers were already turning black, and the whistling of far-off factory hooters was lost in the rain.

Two chauffeur-driven automobiles approached with water spilling back from the wipers and cleaving down the hoods. They were black automobiles, though the rain gave them a deep-blue shine. They were high-bodied, carried special insignia, the radiator caps were nickel-plated. Grille to bumper they came into the cobbled yard and parked near the pump. The doors and windows remained shut, the engines continued to run; for half an hour the cars stood shedding the rain and no one alighted. Finally, when the rain failed to slacken, two men wearing waterproofs and bowlers got down—small men, Violet Lane detectives.

Wiping their faces with damp handkerchiefs, they went together down the wide walk between the rows of stalls, and the black cars followed at a little distance, low gears running smoothly as music boxes. The odor of rain-washed bridges drifted up to mix with dead smells of the stables: spread out from here were the gravel heaps, the leaking slate roofs and single rooms and roots and, farther on, the jewels, the places of execution, the familiar castle walls. All wet, all pitched in gloom. The two men knew this rain. It meant tea with lemon, housemaids out of mood, drops of water on spike fences and lickings for their boys. It meant women going it upright beneath the bridges and tall blue sergeants caped and miserable, helpless on all the corners. And it meant a dampness in the trousers that no coal fire could dry.

They stopped together at the stall door. They wiped their faces. They watched the water coming down the crevices in the wood, they inspected the hinges, the type of nail used, made note of a dead wasp caught on a green splinter. Then one pulled open the door and they stepped inside, looked up at the rafters, down at the straw, touched the wall planking with the very ends of their fingers, prodded the straw with their black shoes. And squatted and carefully took away the straw until Hencher's legs were uncovered to the knees. One fetched a black rubber ground sheet from his car; they rolled and sealed up the body. The straw would have to be sifted through a screen.

They posted one of the drivers to guard the stall until the laboratory boys could take the body and the straw. The driver stood at attention, a lonely man in an empty stable with his shoulders black with rain and his chin pulled into his collar. He smelled the burden on the other side of the wood. It was darker now and the rain heavier.

Between the two gently rocking cars—machines heavy with the sounds of their engines and streaming black—the Violet Lane detectives faced each other, stood close together and stared into each other's eyes. The mortuary bells were ringing and the water was coming off the brims of the bowlers.

"It's never nice to find these fellows in the rain."

"Well, I expect we'd best get on with it."

"We could trace him through the laundries."

"And there are always the tobacco shops, of course."

"Right. I've made out well before with the laundries."

"Go to it then. I'll try the shops. . . ."

And in gloom, with the bells stroking and the wipers establishing the uncomfortable rhythm of the hour, the two wet men withdrew to the cars and in slow procession quit the sooty stables in Highland Green, drove separately through vacant city streets to uncover the particulars of this crime.

New Directions Paperbooks—A Partial Listing

Walter Abish, *In the Future Perfect*. NDP440.
How German Is It. NDP508.
Ilango Adigal, *Shilapa-dikaram*. NDP162.
Alain, *The Gods*. NDP382.
Wayne Andrews. *Voltaire*. NDP519.
David Antin, *Talking at the Boundaries*. NDP388.
Tuning. NDP570.
G. Apollinaire, *Selected Writings*.† NDP310.
C. J. Bangs, *The Bones of the Earth*. NDP563.
Djuna Barnes, *Nightwood*. NDP98.
Charles Baudelaire, *Flowers of Evil*.† NDP71,
Paris Spleen. NDP294.
R. P. Blackmur, *Studies in Henry James*, NDP552.
Wolfgang Borchert, *The Man Outside*. NDP319.
Johan Borgen. *Lillelord*. NDP531.
Jorge Luis Borges, *Labyrinths*. NDP186.
E. Brock, *Here. Now. Always*. NDP429.
The River and the Train. NDP478.
Buddha, *The Dhammapada*. NDP188.
Frederick Busch, *Domestic Particulars*. NDP413.
Manual Labor. NDP376.
Ernesto Cardenal, *In Cuba* NDP377.
Hayden Carruth, *For You*. NDP298.
From Snow and Rock, from Chaos. NDP349.
Louis-Ferdinand Céline,
Death on the Installment Plan NDP330.
Journey to the End of the Night. NDP84.
Jean Cocteau, *The Holy Terrors*. NDP212.
Robert Coles, *Irony in the Mind's Life*. NDP459.
Cid Corman, *Livingdying*. NDP289.
Sun Rock Man. NDP318.
Gregory Corso, *Elegiac Feelings*. NDP299.
Herald of the Autochthonic Spirit. NDP522.
Long Live Man. NDP127.
Robert Creeley, *Hello*. NDP451.
Later. NDP488.
Mirrors, NDP559.
Edward Dahlberg, *Reader*. NDP246.
Because I Was Flesh. NDP227.
René Daumal. *Rasa*. NDP530.
Osamu Dazai, *The Setting Sun*. NDP258.
No Longer Human. NDP357.
Coleman Dowell, *Mrs. October* . . . NDP368.
Robert Duncan, *Bending the Bow*. NDP255.
Ground Work. NDP571, The Opening of the
Field. NDP356, *Roots and Branches*. NDP275.
Richard Eberhart, *The Long Reach*. NDP565.
Selected Poems. NDP198.
E. F. Edinger, *Melville's Moby-Dick*. NDP460.
Wm. Empson, *7 Types of Ambiguity*. NDP204.
Some Versions of Pastoral. NDP92.
Wm. Everson, *The Residual Years*. NDP263.
Lawrence Ferlinghetti, *Her*. NDP88.
A Coney Island of the Mind. NDP74.
Endless Life. NDP516.
The Mexican Night. NDP300.
The Secret Meaning of Things. NDP268.
Starting from San Francisco. NDP220.
Ronald Firbank. *Five Novels*. NDP518.
F. Scott Fitzgerald, *The Crack-up*. NDP54.
Robert Fitzgerald, *Spring Shade*. NDP311.
Gustave Flaubert, *Dictionary*. NDP230.
C. Froula, *Guide to Ezra Pound's Selected Poems*.
NDP548.
Gandhi, *Gandhi on Non-Violence*. NDP197.
Goethe, *Faust*, Part I. NDP70.
Henry Green. *Back*. NDP517.
Allen Grossman, *The Woman on the Bridge
Over the Chicago River*. NDP473.
Of The Great House. NDP535.
Lars Gustafsson, *The Death of a Beekeeper*.
NDP523.
The Tennis Players. NDP551.
John Hawkes, *The Beetle Leg*. NDP239.
The Blood Oranges. NDP338.
The Cannibal. NDP123.
Death Sleep & The Traveler. NDP391.
Second Skin. NDP146.
Travesty. NDP430.
Samuel Hazo. *To Paris*. NDP512.
Thank a Bored Angel. NDP555.
H. D., *End to Torment*. NDP476.
The Gift. NDP546.
Hermetic Definition. NDP343.
HERmione. NDP526.
Tribute to Freud. NDP572.
Trilogy. NDP362.
Robert E. Helbling, *Heinrich von Kleist*, NDP390.
William Herrick. *Love and Terror*. NDP538.
Kill Memory. NDP558.
Hermann Hesse, *Siddhartha*. NDP65.
Vicente Huidobro. *Selected Poetry*. NDP520.
C. Isherwood, *All the Conspirators*. NDP480.
The Berlin Stories. NDP134.
Ledo Ivo, *Snake's Nest*. NDP521.
Alfred Jarry, *Ubu Roi*. NDP105.
Robinson Jeffers, *Cawdor and Media*. NDP293.
James Joyce, *Stephen Hero*. NDP133.
James Joyce/Finnegans Wake. NDP331.
Franz Kafka, *Amerika*. NDP117.
Bob Kaufman,
The Ancient Rain. NDP514.
Solitudes Crowded with Loneliness. NDP199.
Kenyon Critics, *G. M. Hopkins*. NDP355.
H. von Kleist, *Prince Friedrich*. NDP462.
Elaine Kraf, *The Princess of 72nd St*. NDP494.
Shimpei Kusano, *Asking Myself, Answering Myself*.
NDP566.
P. Lal, *Great Sanskrit Plays*. NDP142.
Davide Lajolo, *An Absurd Vice*. NDP545.
Lautréamont, *Maldoror*. NDP207.
Irving Layton, *Selected Poems*. NDP431.
Christine Lehner. *Expecting*. NDP544.
Denise Levertov, *Candles in Babylon*. NDP533.
Collected Earlier. NDP475.
Footprints. NDP344.
The Freeing of the Dust. NDP401.
Light Up The Cave. NDP525.
Life in the Forest. NDP461.
Poems 1960–1967. NDP549.
The Poet in the World. NDP363.
Relearning the Alphabet. NDP290.
To Stay Alive. NDP325.
Harry Levin, *James Joyce*. NDP87.
Memories of The Moderns. NDP539.
Li Ch'ing-chao, *Complete Poems*. NDP492.
Enrique Lihn, *The Dark Room*.† NDP452.
Garciá Lorca, *Deep Song*. NDP503.
Five Plays. NDP232.
The Public & Play Without a Title. NDP561.
Selected Letters. NDP557.
Selected Poems.† NDP114.
Three Tragedies. NDP52.
Michael McClure, *Antechamber*. NDP455.
Fragments of Perseus. NDP554.
Jaguar Skies. NDP400.
Josephine: The Mouse Singer. NDP496.
Carson McCullers, *The Member of the
Wedding*. (Playscript) NDP153.
Stephen Mallarmé.† *Selected Poetry and
Prose*. NDP529.
Thomas Merton, *Asian Journal*. NDP394.
Collected Poems. NDP504.
Gandhi on Non-Violence. NDP197.
News Seeds of Contemplation. NDP337.
Selected Poems. NDP85.
The Way of Chuang Tzu. NDP276.
The Wisdom of the Desert. NDP295.
Zen and the Birds of Appetite. NDP261.
Henry Miller, *The Air-Conditioned Nightmare*.
NDP302.
Big Sur & The Oranges. NDP161.
The Books in My Life. NDP280.
The Colossus of Maroussi. NDP75.
The Cosmological Eye. NDP109.
From Your Capricorn Friend. NDP568.
The Smile at the Foot of the Ladder. NDP386.
Stand Still Like the Hummingbird. NDP236.

The Time of the Assassins. NDP115.
Y. Mishima, *Confessions of a Mask.* NDP253.
Death in Midsummer. NDP215.
Eugenio Montale, *It Depends.*† NDP507.
New Poems. NDP410.
Selected Poems.† NDP193.
Paul Morand, *Fancy Goods/Open All Night.* NDP567.
Vladimir Nabokov, *Nikolai Gogol.* NDP78.
Laughter in the Dark. NDP470.
The Real Life of Sebastian Knight. NDP432.
P. Neruda, *The Captain's Verses.*† NDP345.
Residence on Earth.† NDP340.
New Directions in Prose & Poetry (Anthology). Available from #17 forward. #48, Fall 1984.
Robert Nichols, *Arrival.* NDP437.
Exile. NDP485. *Garh City.* NDP450.
Harditts in Sawna. NDP470.
Charles Olson. *Selected Writings.* NDP231.
Toby Olson, *The Life of Jesus.* NDP417.
Seaview. NDP532.
George Oppen, *Collected Poems.* NDP418.
István Örkeny. *The Flower Show/ The Toth Family.* NDP536
Wilfred Owen, *Collected Poems.* NDP210.
Nicanor Parra, *Poems and Antipoems.*† NDP242.
Boris Pasternak, *Safe Conduct.* NDP77.
Kenneth Patchen. *Aflame and Afun.* NDP292.
Because It Is. NDP83.
But Even So. NDP265.
Collected Poems. NDP284.
Hallelujah Anyway. NDP219.
In Quest of Candlelighters. NDP334.
Selected Poems. NDP160.
Octavio Paz, *Configurations.*† NDP303.
A Draft of Shadows.† NDP489.
Eagle or Sun?† NDP422.
Selected Poems. NDP574.
St. John Perse.† *Selected Poems.* NDP545.
Plays for a New Theater. (Anth.) NDP216.
J. A. Porter, *Eelgrass.* NDP438.
Ezra Pound, *ABC of Reading.* NDP89.
Collected Early Poems. NDP540.
Confucius. NDP285.
Confucius to Cummings. (Anth.) NDP126.
Gaudier Brzeska. NDP372.
Guide to Kulchur, NDP257.
Literary Essays. NDP250.
Selected Cantos. NDP304.
Selected Letters 1907-1941. NDP317.
Selected Poems. NDP66.
The Spirit of Romance. NDP266.
Translations.† (Enlarged Edition) NDP145.
Raymond Queneau, *The Bark Tree.* NDP314.
Exercises in Style. NDP513.
The Sunday of Life. NDP433.
We Always Treat Women Too Well. NDP515.
Mary de Rachewiltz, *Ezra Pound.* NDP405.
John Crowe Ransom, *Beating the Bushes.* NDP324.
Raja Rao, *Kanthapura.* NDP224.
Herbert Read, *The Green Child.* NDP208.
P. Reverdy, *Selected Poems.*† NDP346.
Kenneth Rexroth, *Collected Longer Poems.* NDP309. *Collected Shorter.* NDP243.
The Morning Star. NDP490.
New Poems. NDP383.
100 More Poems from the Chinese. NDP308.
100 More Poems from the Japanese. NDP420.
100 Poems from the Chinese. NDP192.
100 Poems from the Japanese.† NDP147.
Women Poets of China. NDP528.
Women Poets of Japan. NDP527
Rainer Maria Rilke, *Poems from The Book of Hours.* NDP408.
Possibility of Being. (Poems). NDP436.
Where Silence Reigns. (Prose). NDP464.
Arthur Rimbaud, *Illuminations.*† NDP56.
Season in Hell & Drunken Boat.† NDP97.
Edouard Roditi, *Delights of Turkey.* NDP445.
Jerome Rothenberg, *That Dada Strain.* NDP550.
Poland/1931. NDP379.
Vienna Blood. NDP498.
Saigyo,† *Mirror for the Moon.* NDP465.
Saikaku Ihara. *The Life of an Amorous Woman.* NDP270.
St. John of the Cross, *Poems.*† NDP341.
Jean-Paul Sartre, *Nausea.* NDP82.
The Wall (Intimacy). NDP272.
Delmore Schwartz, *Selected Poems.* NDP241.
In Dreams Begin Responsibilities. NDP454.
K. Shiraishi, *Seasons of Sacred Lust.* NDP453.
Stevie Smith, *Collected Poems.* NDP562.
Selected Poems, NDP159.
Gary Snyder, *The Back Country.* NDP249.
Earth House Hold. NDP267.
The Real Work. NDP499.
Regarding Wave. NDP306.
Turtle Island. NDP381.
Gustaf Sobin, *The Earth as Air.* NDP569.
Enid Starkie, *Rimbaud.* NDP254.
Robert Steiner, *Bathers.* NDP495
Stendhal, *The Telegraph.* NDP108.
Jules Supervielle, *Selected Writings.*† NDP209.
Nathaniel Tarn, *Lyrics . . . Bride of God.* NDP391.
Dylan Thomas, *Adventures in the Skin Trade.* NDP183.
A Child's Christmas in Wales. NDP181.
Collected Poems 1934-1952. NDP316.
Portrait of the Artist as a Young Dog. NDP51.
Quite Early One Morning. NDP90.
Rebecca's Daughters. NDP543.
Under Milk Wood. NDP73.
Lionel Trilling. *E. M. Forster.* NDP189.
Martin Turnell. *Baudelaire.* NDP336.
Rise of the French Novel. NDP474.
Paul Valéry, *Selected Writings.*† NDP184.
Elio Vittorini, *Women of Messina.* NDP365.
Vernon Watkins, *Selected Poems.* NDP221.
Nathanael West, *Miss Lonelyhearts & Day of the Locust.* NDP125.
J. Wheelwright, *Collected Poems.* NDP544.
J. Williams, *An Ear in Bartram's Tree.* NDP335.
Tennessee Williams, *Camino Real,* NDP301.
Cat on a Hot Tin Roof. NDP398.
Clothes for a Summer Hotel. NDP556.
Dragon Country. NDP287.
The Glass Menagerie. NDP218.
Hard Candy. NDP225.
In the Winter of Cities. NDP154.
A Lovely Sunday for Creve Coeur. NDP497.
One Arm & Other Stories. NDP237.
Stopped Rocking. NDP575.
A Streetcar Named Desire. NDP501.
Sweet Bird of Youth. NDP409.
Twenty-Seven Wagons Full of Cotton. NDP217.
Vieux Carré. NDP482.
William Carlos Williams.
The Autobiography. NDP223.
The Buildup. NDP259.
The Farmers' Daughters. NDP106.
I Wanted to Write a Poem. NDP469.
Imaginations. NDP329.
In the American Grain. NDP53.
In the Money. NDP240.
Paterson. Complete. NDP152.
Pictures form Brueghel. NDP118.
Selected Poems. NDP131.
White Mule. NDP226.
Yes, Mrs. Williams. NDP534.
Yvor Winters, *E. A. Robinson.* NDP326.
Wisdom Books: *Ancient Egyptians,* NDP467. *Early Buddhists,* NDP444; *English Mystics,* NDP466; *Forest* (Hindu), NDP414; *Spanish Mystics,* NDP442; *St. Francis,* NDP477; *Sufi,* NDP424; *Taoists,* NDP509; *Wisdom of the Desert,* NDP295; *Zen Masters,* NDP415.

† Bilingual